THE

STRAWBERRY

WINE

CLUB

A Pacific Grove Mystery

Jeanne Marie Olin

Cover design, book design, typeset, layout by Barbara Quin

Cover photo insert, Monterey Bay, by Jeanne Marie Olin.

Heart wine glass clipart by Shutterstock via publicdomainpictures.net, public domain images from Bing Images.

Chapter-end butterfly clipart by GDJ, openclipart.org, public domain images from Bing Images.

ISBN-10: 1534624619

ISBN-13: 978-1534624610

Publication creative and technical assistance provided by *GSP-Assist*, a service of

Great Spirit Publishing

Springfield, Missouri
greatspiritpublishing@yahoo.com

Published in the USA.

DEDICATION

To Jim, Tod, Janine, Chris, Claudia, Diego,
Luna, Noella, and Isabelle Olin,
the members of The Strawberry Wine Club,
and my friends at the Monterey Bay Aquarium.

And to Dear Saint Jude.

Autumn is a beautiful time in Pacific Grove, a small town on the Central Coast of California. Scarecrows welcome customers into cute shops and inviting restaurants along Lighthouse Avenue and the Butterfly Parade welcomes Monarch butterflies back to their winter home.

Jessie Anthony smiled as she hurried to meet Joan Savage at Juice and Java. She wanted to be there before the beginning of the Butterfly Parade. Children wearing Monarch butterfly wings were already jostling for position along the parade route. She anticipated a fun morning and looked forward to meeting with Joan to plan festivities for the Strawberry Wine Club's first fall meeting. How could she have known that she was rushing into a web of conspiracy involving aquatic trafficking, human trafficking, and even murder?

Come join the Strawberry Wine Club as they turn tragedy into charity and sadness into romance. Don't be late for the party!

PREFACE

A LITTLE HISTORY

Pacific Grove is a small town on the beautiful Central Coast of California known as "The Last Home Town." It has been heralded in travel websites and magazines as a beautiful seaside town known for its views, moderate climate, marine sanctuary and quaint cottages. The residents of Pacific Grove take great pride in their town and its intriguing history.

Point Pinos Lighthouse was built in 1855. It remains to this date as the oldest continuously operating lighthouse on the West Coast. In 1875 the Pacific Grove Retreat Association was founded and soon a Methodist seaside resort and campgrounds were established on property that would become Pacific Grove.

In 1939, Pacific Grove earned international attention by passing an ordinance that made it a misdemeanor to molest a butterfly. One should note that the butterfly remains a very important resident of this small community. In October every year Pacific Grove's Monarch Butterfly sanctuary awaits the return of the butterflies that make Pacific Grove their winter home. The return of the butterflies is celebrated by the annual Butterfly Parade.

The Strawberry Wine Club formed in 2014 when a group of ladies in this beautiful small town found they shared a love of mystery, adventure, philanthropy, spirituality, and fun. They started meeting to participate in sparkling conversation, sparkling wine and water, and a bit of Strawberry Wine from a rare French recipe.

Enjoy!

CHAPTER 1

RETURN OF THE BUTTERFLIES

Joan and Jessie surveyed the parade route as they sat perched on their stools in the corner window of Juice and Java. The autumn air had turned cool on October 3, 2015, and sipping coffee in the warmth of one of their favorite coffee/tea/wine bars seemed appropriate.

"We could get up and go outside to watch the parade, but I am so comfortable here," Jessie said after pointing out the local kindergarten class dressed as butterflies.

"I don't have a grandchild in the parade. I am very content to watch from here," Joan smiled. "I was just thinking that, like the monarch butterfly, many of the members of the Strawberry Wine Club return to Pacific Grove for the winter. I am looking forward to their return. Our club meetings will be larger soon."

"I will keep my eyes open for some beautiful strawberries for some strawberry wine. We need to have an official meeting of the Club soon. I want to get together and start putting our recipes together for our booklet. It would also be great to have the recipes booklet in time for a

Christmas gift for our families," Jessie added.

Jessie's face showed concern. She scowled at another customer. "Joan, I am sorry but that man is starting to annoy me. I wish that when people have intimate, tense conversations on their cell phones they would move away from other groups." Jessie was eyeing a scruffy looking man who was raising his voice in anger and shouting into his phone. "No matter how hard I try to ignore that conversation I find it impossible to block it."

"Let's get out of here. I'll see you tomorrow." Joan got up and nodded to Jessie. "We'll go on the Historic Walking Tour tomorrow."

As Jessie walked the short few blocks back to her home she smiled at the groups of children who had just completed the parade. She glanced back toward Juice and Java in time to see the man with the cell phone rush out. He pushed through the groups of children, continuing to shout at the phone as he made his way down Lighthouse Avenue.

Jessie smiled as she passed a shop with a scarecrow in its doorway and a jaunty hat on its head. The center divider of the street was piled high with hay and pumpkins were scattered throughout the bails. Banners hung from the lampposts cheering the return of the butterflies.

Joe and I moved here four years ago. I love it here. Pacific Grove has so many fun events. I am awed by the ocean I can almost see from our porch and the pink ice plant that blooms in the spring along the shore. Above all else, I love the warm and friendly people. People move here from all over the country because of the rare beauty of these shores and bring with them special talents and new ideas.

*****

Sunday was a sparkling autumn day, just perfect for a walk that would feature the lovely Victorian homes built along the rocky shore. Joan and Jessie enjoyed listening to the tour leader as he described the pretty homes and the interesting people who built them a century ago.

"I love hearing information about Julia Platt. What a woman! I have heard quite a bit about her at the Monterey Aquarium. I don't think the

Bay would be what it is today without her strong conservation ideals." Jessie was an Aquarium volunteer.

"What's going on at Lover's Point? The fire department and police seem to be clearing an area," Joan said from the rear of the tour, looking back at Lover's Point Beach. The tour leader continued to move the group down the street in the opposite direction. Joan hurried to catch up and listen to the remainder of the tour.

*****

That evening Jessie and Joe decided to stop for a cocktail after picking up groceries. The evening was particularly beautiful and Jessie suggested that they enjoy the view from the Beach House on Lover's Point Beach. Usually at this time of year there are still plenty of divers and swimmers around the beach. This evening, however, the beach was particularly quiet. Jessie and Joe had not stopped at the Beach House during the very busy summer and were warmly welcomed by the friendly bartender.

"What have you two been up to? I haven't seen too much of you lately," Bill the bartender asked.

"We've been doing a little bit of cruising and a lot of just enjoying summer," Jessie answered. "This seems rather quiet for a beautiful fall Sunday evening. Is there anything special going on?"

Bill shook his head. "I haven't been here very long, but I understand there was a police presence here earlier this afternoon."

"Haven't you heard? A body washed up here this afternoon. The victim was dressed in a wetsuit," a customer on Jessie's right joined the conversation.

Joe entered the discussion. "To the best of your knowledge, was the victim identified? The sea is like a bathtub this afternoon. I wouldn't think there would be much difficulty in swimming around here or for that matter in boating around here."

"No, I got my information third-hand. All I know is that no resuscitation attempt was made. I think the victim was gone by the time the body washed up onto the shore. It does seem rather unusual on such a calm afternoon. Perhaps the victim had a medical emergency. I really know very little."

Joe looked puzzled. "I have always been told that you never turn your back on the ocean. In this case the victim was in a wetsuit so one would imagine he or she was in the water. My guess would be that there was a medical emergency. There is no reason to think there was foul play."

"I am sure we will hear more about this event. Joan mentioned seeing the police and fire department on the beach when we were taking our history walk. It is just so very sad," Jessie commented.

CHAPTER II

A MEETING OF THE CLUB

It was a particularly beautiful day. Jessie had walked along the bike trail that runs along the bay from Pacific Grove to Monterey. The sun was warm and she could see several otters having their breakfasts, banging the shells of their entrees along rocks they held onto.

She met Joe for coffee at the Plaza Hotel. They discussed the story she heard while volunteering at the Monterey Bay Aquarium the day before. She had heard that the diver that washed up on Lover's Point on the previous Saturday had not been identified. She decided that the Strawberry Wine Club should know about this, therefore, a meeting was called. I should explain here that meetings of the club were called for almost any reason on a beautiful day.

The Strawberry Wine Club held a meeting at Juice and Java on October 8, 2015. Members present included Jessie, Joan, Mary, LaVerne, and Mickey.

Joan remembered the scene she observed on the historical walk. She had not heard anything about the accident.

"I imagine the diver was inexperienced and from out of the area. I am surprised that, at this point, no one has been reported missing," Joan said, taking a sip of her tea.

"I am just not that sure that drowning was an accident," Jessie sipped her merlot. "I talked to a friend of mine who is a very experienced diver. She apparently had discussions with other divers in the area. There appears to be some foul play involved but I am not sure she had any real facts. At any rate, she would not elaborate on the fact that she was not sure the drowning was an accident."

Mary laughed. "Jessie, you are just looking for a plot for your next novel. You did mention that you were writing a novel that would take place in Pacific Grove, or at least on the Monterey Peninsula. This event would help you in your search for a plot. I think…" Mary stopped mid-sentence.

Jessie and Joan both looked in the same direction as Mary. He was absolutely glaring at Jessie! It was him, the man from the day of the parade. Jesse froze. *Who is he? Why is he looking at me with such hate? What is it about him that frightens me so?*

He slammed down his cup. He did not look away from Jessie as he stood up. He gave Jessie a look of unmistakable disdain. He then turned and walked out the door as he reached for his cell phone.

Mickey, who had her back to the action, shook her head. "What is wrong with all of you? Joan, you are not even drinking wine. You all look as if you've seen an unfriendly ghost."

Jesse looked at Joan and Mary. "What was that all about? Joan, isn't that the guy from Saturday who was so rude on his cell phone? Am I being super-sensitive?"

Joan nodded, "That was the man from Saturday that would not put down his phone."

Mary chimed in. "You are not being super-sensitive. I don't think he likes you very much. I wonder what he heard. He obviously didn't like what he heard. He also obviously didn't like you."

"I know I live only a few blocks from here, but I think I may need a ride home," Jesse took another sip of her wine. "For some reason, he really frightens me. That being said, I am going to try to get more information with regard to the drowning."

"Sorry I am late," Pat joined the group. She had been volunteering at the Point Pinos Lighthouse. "We had some interesting visitors that were enjoying the lighthouse. I didn't want to rush them through. I love the place so much and enjoy sharing the history with interested guests."

"You are definitely not too late for a little conversation. I think this is a great time to plan a little party for when our snow bird friends return to Pacific Grove," Mary said, who was great at planning parties. "What do you all think about a party to discuss our various vacations during the summer? Everyone has visited such great places. I would love to see pictures. We could plan on it at one of our houses."

The conversation continued in a much more upbeat manner. After some planning and a lot of laughing, Jesse asked Pat to drop her off. She told Pat about the drowning. Pat nodded in agreement at Jesse's suggestion that she felt perhaps the drowning was not an accident.

"I talked to some of the docents at Point Pinos today. They mentioned that there was an ongoing investigation. This, of course, is not unusual in matters such as drownings. It does seem rather unusual that no one has reported anyone missing at this point. It is so sad when something of this sort happens. It does seem strange that the victim appears to be experienced, judging from the equipment he was wearing."

"You seem to have more information than I do. I wasn't sure of the sex of the victim." Jessie carefully listened. She could see the beginning of a fascinating story.

CHAPTER III

THE OCEAN'S BOUNTY

B rad was filled with awe as he stood staring out over Monterey Bay. It was unusually warm for an August day on the Monterey Peninsula. He sat down on a huge rock and dug his toes into the warm sand. The sun was beginning its descent into the pink waters and created a fairyland of sparkling water and pink clouds overhead. He stared into the distance and dreamed. He felt at one with the nature of his surroundings. He knew the ocean's surface beauty as well as the kelp forests and thriving life in its depths. He thought about his past. He thought about a beautiful time in his life and a beautiful person in his life.

Brad had grown to manhood in a small town in Contra Costa County to the east of San Francisco. He loved swimming in the ocean, diving and any water sport he could find. He felt salt water was somehow mixed into his blood and that he needed it to survive.

When it came time to attend a university, Brad chose Cal Poly in San Luis Obispo. He certainly had what it takes to be a great engineer and the studies offered by Cal Poly were second to none. He could not deny, however, that the location of the university and its closeness to the sea helped to persuade him. After he enrolled he would head for one of the beaches surrounding the area at any opportunity.

Brad also began heading a little north to Santa Cruz when he had a little time off from his studies. Surfing was an art form in the water off Santa Cruz and he felt he needed to master the art. He began close friendships with other surfers in the area. His quick smile and adventurous attitude soon attracted a small group of followers who liked to watch the surfers perfect their craft. Belle, a student from UCSC, liked watching him on her walks along the beach.

"Hey, slow down. I've noticed you for a couple of weeks. I've watched you walk along the beach from the top of a couple of waves which is probably why I didn't ride them too well," Brad said as he waved and smiled at Belle. "I could use a cup of java or, better still, a hot chocolate and a little conversation with a pretty girl."

A couple of Brad's friends mocked him. "What a pickup line! Is that the best you can do, Brad? You watched her from the top of a wave? Please, be a little more original."

Belle was enjoying herself immensely. She had mentioned the sandy-haired surfer to her suite mates. "I don't think there is such a thing as an unattractive surfer," she had told them. It was fun meeting him after watching him for weeks.

"I would love a hot chocolate," she said, adjusting her straw sun visor. "The sun is warm but the breeze has just enough chill that a hot chocolate would be awesome." She took off her sunglasses to reveal her beautiful blue eyes and long lashes. "You lead the way."

Brad and Belle saw each other as often as possible over the next few months. They began talking about the future and their mutual love of the sea. Belle was studying the conservation of the oceans. She wasn't a surfer but loved swimming in the ocean. Her future plans included working with a conservation program. She volunteered at the Monterey Bay Aquarium as often as possible with her academic schedule.

At the end of the school year Brad was offered a job diving in the Gulf of Mexico. He would actually work for oil companies, which didn't thrill him; however, his salary was terrific. Brad and Belle parted. They planned on seeing each other at the beginning of the school year. They were both young. Neither of them wanted to rush their relationship. After all, Brad would only be away a few months. He really needed the money he would be paid. They had cell phone numbers. They would keep in touch.

Unfortunately, life sometimes doesn't go the way we plan. Brad needed to stay longer to earn more money and would miss a whole academic year. Belle would graduate sooner than expected. She would enter the Peace Corps and would not return to the Monterey area for more than two years. The two would lose touch of each other. They would not, however, stop thinking about each other.

On that August day, as Brad looked over the Monterey Bay, he thought about his decision to stay in the Gulf area for an extra year. He thought about a beautiful girl with blue eyes in Santa Cruz. He was reminded of her warmth. He had not witnessed such beauty for some time and he yearned to be with her again. She was gone.

He closed his eyes as the sun sunk into the sea. *I just didn't realize how special she was. Please give me another chance. I am in the middle of paradise and I feel so alone.*

Brad had returned to Cal Poly and received a post-graduate degree. He had searched Santa Cruz for Belle but it was to no avail. She had left a year before he returned and tracing her whereabouts was difficult. Their mutual friends had also left. He walked the streets of the seaside town. Everything was the same. Everything was different.

He had left the university but he had not left the area. He was offered a job in the area which took advantage of his unique talents. His engineering skills were excellent plus his knowledge of the ocean was impressive. Surfing, diving, and swimming in it had taught him many lessons. He was happy to be able to use all his skills in his employment. He was happy in his career, but he needed and wanted to be happy in his personal life as well.

*****

Belle looked out over the bay. She was perched on a bench in the Great Tide Pool area of the Monterey Bay Aquarium. She had just watched the summer show put on by actors from the Aquarium that told the story of the history of the Monterey Bay. The crowd had dispersed and Belle had the space she needed to dream a little of the past.

The Peace Corps had been fun. She certainly learned a lot regarding the culture and needs of the village in which she worked. Her experience reinforced her desire to work with the environment. Upon her return to the Monterey area she took post graduate classes and was fortunate enough to obtain work with an affiliate of the Monterey Bay Aquarium. She was passionate about her work. Her career was everything she had ever hoped it would be.

Her personal life, however, had not been so great. Belle missed Brad. She had been annoyed when he casually told her that he was remaining in the New Orleans area to continue his employment with the oil companies. She had mixed emotions with regards to oil companies drilling offshore and she certainly couldn't understand how Brad could just expect her to wait. He promised nothing. She had felt she needed to move on.

She moved on to the Peace Corps. Her decision was made very swiftly. She had graduated midterm the year Brad was in New Orleans. She was recruited by the Peace Corps and she jumped at the chance of working with such an admirable organization. She had thrown herself into her work and did not look back, not at first.

Sitting on that bench that summer day, she looked back. She remembered his tanned body, easy smile, and the warmth of his arms. But it was too late. He was gone. She did not know if he ever graduated from Cal Poly. He might be an executive at an oil company that drilled in the Gulf of Mexico. He might be diving for abalone somewhere. She had thought they had a mutual love of conservation and the environment. Her yearning for him after he left had been so passionate, but then… Life goes on.

Some memories do not fade. Some memories haunt us passionately and persistently. They remain somewhere behind our eyes when we close them. They reoccur at the sound of a particular song or voice or laugh. Then we have got to look back. Then we have to have regrets. When we truly love, our love is not just a memory. It is an artist that molds us into the person we become. We can become bitter and shut out the world. The wise realize that the more love they have had the more love they can give. Belle decided that she would be happy and would love. She knew the choice was hers to make.

Sounds of the children participating in the diving program in the Great Tide Pool brought Belle out of her reverie. She smiled at the Aquarium divers that would be working with the young divers. She waved at the children and moved out of the way of anxious parents trying to take photos of their offspring.

The summer was in full swing at the Monterey Aquarium.

CHAPTER IV

A MYSTERY

Jessie walked along the sunny bike trail, admiring her view. It was Sunday, October 11, 2015. Jessie was due at her shift at the Monterey Bay Aquarium at 8:30 a.m. Her walk along the trail was a bonus to working as an Aquarium volunteer. She enjoyed the fall weather with a hint of cooler times in the early morning. The morning had started off sunny and then puffs of fog drifted in and out of the Bay. The day was going to be perfect. Joe would be busy watching the series of football games on television that day along with the baseball playoff games. He would not even miss her presence until the end of her shift.

The guide lounge was packed with the first shift volunteers. The enrichment topic of the day was climate change. Jesse noticed Belle sitting at the end of a table listening to the lecture. She continued to volunteer at the Aquarium even though she worked full-time for an affiliate of the Aquarium. Weekends worked best for Belle so Jessie had the opportunity to catch up on her adventures on a regular basis. Belle had started scuba diving and shared many of her underwater photos and videos with the aquarium staff and volunteers. She had been fully certified for at least 70 feet. She actually helped in the Aquarium tanks, both to help clean the tanks and to feed the fish at the various shows.

Jesse was fascinated with the underwater beauty and life she watched on the videos. She appreciated the fragility of the ocean and was proud to be a part of promoting its conservation. This morning, however, she found it difficult to concentrate on the enrichment. Jessie wondered if anyone knew anything new regarding the diver that had washed up on Lover's Point.

Jesse had talked to a few of her shift-mates before the program began and learned nothing. No announcements had been made. This seemed to be unusual. Identification should have been made by this point.

"Please make sure you have your belongings with you because you will be on the floor directly after our field trip," the enrichment leader smiled as she clicked off the video regarding climate change. "We are going to have the opportunity to view some of our rare coral exhibits. I think you will enjoy viewing these tanks before our guests arrive. The Monterey Bay Aquarium is an expert in the care of these exhibits. We have been used by the U.S. Fish and Wildlife Service to actually hold evidence that would be used in cases involving aquarium traffickers."

Jesse suddenly became very interested in the enrichment. She loved field trips within the Aquarium before it officially opened. The atmosphere was completely different when there was no noise from guests and the tanks were so close. This interaction was a fantastic benefit of volunteering at the Aquarium.

"Is that an angel shark there? I can see an outline in the sand that resembles one," Jessie said, staring into the tank in the Ocean's Edge section of the Aquarium. "Usually, I cannot find the angel shark. They really dig under the sand and just don't move enough to be noticed."

"It sure is an angel shark," Belle said as she joined Jesse on the enrichment tour. "Look at the huge bass over there. I think it is anxious for breakfast. It is really impressive, zipping around, looking for adventure and food. We had better catch up with the rest of the group. They are going behind the scenes."

The leader was holding the inner door open for the tour to enter the area that was off limits for guests. The lighting in the hallway was much brighter than in the Kelp Forest, although the tanks within were kept in the proper dim light.

"The coral over there is so beautiful. The color is so vibrant. I really love the mixture of lavender and bright pink in that colony. When I was younger, I did not realize that coral was actually living invertebrates. I thought they were some sort of stone," Jesse said.

The tour leader heard Jessie's comment. "That is not unusual, Jessie. Coral jewelry was popular for years. So much coral was destroyed that conservation groups have formed for its protection. It is against the law to remove coral in many areas of the ocean. It is worth billions of dollars because of tourist trade and many related issues. Aquatic trafficking deals in coral as well as protected species of fish. The tanks over there contain coral that was taken from protected areas. It will be used as evidence in prosecuting traffickers."

Jessie and Belle enjoyed that enrichment and hurried to their volunteer areas to be in time for the Aquarium opening.

"Belle, have you heard anything about the drowning victim off Lover's Point?" Jessie asked.

"As a matter of fact, yesterday, I was told that the victim did not drown. Medical tests showed that he was dead when he went into the water. I don't know if he died of natural causes or if he was murdered. It is really very strange," Belle said and shook her head. "He was dressed in a diving suit. He must have come from another area. None of the diving clubs or businesses is missing members or employees. The police have run all the usual investigations and yet they have not come up with identification. If he was diving legally, he would have to have a PADI, the international certification. It is strange that he could not be identified in some manner."

"Let's get together for coffee or wine soon. I want to hear about your adventures and any new and exciting men in your life," Jessie said as they stopped at the information desk, where she volunteered.

Belle smiled, "Adventure and friends are wonderful. As far as any romantic interests, I have none. I am thinking of going on a website. I definitely need some help. Let me know when you want to get together." Belle waved as she hurried to her post.

*****

Jessie met Joe after her shift. "Belle told me that the victim that washed up on Lover's Point did not drown. He was dead before he hit the water. Doesn't that sound like foul play? Did you see anything about the case on the news?"

"No, I haven't heard anything. Unfortunately, there is very little local news on Sundays between games. Now, if you are interested in the football or baseball scores, I can be much more helpful. I'll let you watch the news briefly at 5:30 p.m."

"You're too kind! I'll talk to Joan when I get home. I know Jack was watching football but hopefully she has able to have some contact with the world besides what she could find out on ESPN. Thanks for lunch."

The 5:30 p.m. news confirmed Belle's report. The victim had not drowned. His body was badly battered. It was not known if those injures came from the sea. The cause of death, however, was from a stab wound. No identification had been made. The victim was Asian and appeared to be in his late thirties. No other information was given.

Jesse was unable to reach Joan. Both Jesse and Joan were scheduled to work at the church the next morning in a government-sponsored food program. Jesse knew they could meet afterwards. *Perhaps this would be a good time for a Strawberry Wine Club meeting.*

The food truck arrived before any clients. There were more volunteers than usual at the hall that Monday morning. Joan and Jessie decided to have coffee after the program. The clients arrived slowly at first but then a rather large group arrived at the same time. Most of the clients were recognized as participating in the program in the past. A group of four young Asian people came in together. They were dressed in clothes that could only be called rags. Only one of them, a young girl, spoke English. She was very pretty but also very thin. She indicated that they lived in Pacific Grove. The address she gave was very close to Jessie's home. It was obvious the young girl was uncomfortable giving out that information. She was told, however, that it was necessary in order to receive food as this was a government program. She signed the application form as Lee Hong. She indicated that they had not participated in the program in the past and that they all lived in the same residence.

A mini meeting of The Strawberry Wine Club was held after the end of the food program. Joan had called Mary and Mickey. Jessie called LaVerne and Pat. The six members met at the Coffee Roasters. Jessie wanted to talk to the members with regard to the apparent homicide discovered at Lover's Point. Jessie was interested in a plot for her novel and knew the club members would have some interesting ideas.

The Coffee Roasters was quieter than usual. Coffees and teas and lattes were the drinks of the day. The riddle of the day was on the bar and no one could figure it out. Mickey glanced at the answer on the back and groaned. "Don't even try to figure it out," she laughed.

"Joan, I was wondering what you thought about the young Asian group that came in this morning. They really looked like they could use some extra help. I told them about the St. Vincent de Paul vouchers. I hope they take advantage of them to get some clothes. I was surprised that they actually had an address," Jessie said as she sipped her latte.

Joan nodded. "They looked like they had big problems. Didn't you mention the address they gave was right around here?"

"Yes, it is in the next block. I am going to walk over after coffee. I am curious as to which house they live in. I wrote down the address." Jessie was always ready for adventure.

The Club discussed the apparent Lover's Point homicide at some length. "Talking about this really bothers me. It's hard to imagine what could have happened. I wish we could find out if the victim was already dead when he got into his diving suit or was put into his diving suit," Jessie puzzled.

"This discussion is starting to depress me. Why don't we start planning a Halloween party? I think we are all in need of a little fun injection," Joan smiled.

"Let's hold that thought. I have a nail appointment in a half an hour. I want time to walk past that house." Jessie pushed back her chair.

"I'll go with you. That group looked so in need. I would like to see the house to see if we can help." Joan joined Jessie.

The house was a very short walk from the coffee shop. It was very much in need of repair. One of the windows was broken and boards were missing from a couple of the outer walls. Joan and Jessie walked up onto the front porch and knocked. "I don't think anyone is home." Joan knocked again on the door. She turned the knob. The door was unlocked. "Hello! Is anybody home?" she called as she pushed the door open.

Jessie looked at Joan as they both walked into the house. "Look at this room! It is all furnished and furnished well. It looks as if we are in some sort of library and dining area. This is amazing after looking at the outside of the house I would never have guessed it was so nice on the inside."

Joan started walking around the room. The sun was streaming through a very dirty window. "The room is dusted and the books are in order. There is china in the cabinet. Let's look in the kitchen. I think that is the room with the broken window. Hello! Is there anyone here?" No one answered. Joan and Jessie continued to the rest of the home.

The kitchen had promises of what might have been. The cabinets and counter tops were charming. They surrounded a small atrium area. Unfortunately, the skylight covering the atrium area was broken as well as the side window. Water had clearly gotten into the house. The kitchen floor was rotting out in several places. Someone had draped plastic sheets around the areas that had water damage. Still the cabinets and counter tops were arranged in a very neat manner and wiped clean. Kitchen towels and utensils were neatly stacked in their assigned areas. Joan and Jessie were puzzled.

They walked into the next room, a bedroom. The large bed was neatly made with a colorful quilt and designer type pillows. The dresser and ornate mirror were in very good condition. Shades were drawn and appeared to also be in working condition. There was a bathroom next to this room that was also in good condition.

"Look at this!" Joan held up a card that rested on the dresser.

Jessie read the card. "It's a card of a real estate agent. I've heard about the Mogg Real Estate Company. Let's call Lorelee Mogg. I wonder if this home is on the market. It seems so odd that the inside of the house is in order except for the kitchen while the outside is a mess. Perhaps the real estate company is trying to stage the house. Let's take a look at the next room. I cannot forget my appointment at the nail salon."

Jessie pushed open the door to the second bedroom. This bedroom was furnished with twin beds. The bed linens were blue and trimmed with white lace. Jessie looked around the room and noticed a bag that was placed in the closet. The bag was a large, black garbage bag. Jessie walked over hesitating for only a moment before she opened it. She shook her head. "The food we gave out to the Asian group is all here except for the cereal bars. They definitely were here. I assume they are planning on coming back. I need to go to my appointment. The real estate company is on the way. I'll stop on the way back."

Joan laughed. "What are you going to say to Lorelee Mogg? 'I found your card in the bedroom of this house I broke into'?"

Jessie shook her head. "No, I will tell her that I am interested in this house. I will ask her to look into its status. I will certainly not mention its guests. I doubt very much that they are invited. I will let you know what I find out."

When Jessie was finished with her nail appointment, she walked over to the Mogg Real Estate Company. She was feeling very unsure of herself when she opened the door of the boutique office. Lorelee Mogg was behind her desk. She smiled at Jessie when Jessie entered the office. "How can I help you? Thanks for coming in on this beautiful day."

"I wondered if you could help me in regard to the house located at 14 Amber Street. It appears to need some fixing up but I think it has possibilities. I was curious as to whether it was on the market."

"As a matter of fact, it is and it is one of our properties. We are in the process of working out some details with the owner. Are you interested in purchasing the property as is? We would, of course, do all the necessary inspections."

"I am really not sure. Are you renting the property at this time?"

Lorelee looked rather surprised at the question. "No, it is not really considered habitable. The owner is not local. The owner has given us full authority with regard to repairs. Are you interested in renting or buying? We have no interest in renting that property but we have other properties available for long time rental. As you know, Pacific Grove is looking to limit its short-term rentals."

"I actually own a home in Pacific Grove. I am just curious about the property."

"I thought you looked familiar. I think I saw your picture with some other ladies in the local paper. Aren't you a member of some sort of wine club?"

Jessie laughed. "Yes, I am Jessie Anthony. I am a member of the Strawberry Wine Club. A couple of us had our picture taken after we completed the pilgrimage from San Carlos Cathedral to the Carmel Mission. We have a lot of fun. My daughter brought home from France a recipe for strawberry wine. I made it for a group of friends and we have been meeting ever since. We meet mostly for fun and conversation. Occasionally, we try to do something for the community."

"That sounds like great fun! Let me know when you are recruiting members."

"I will and I have your card. Thank you for being so helpful." Jessie smiled as she left the office.

She called Joan as soon as she started walking home along Lighthouse. "I don't know what is going on. I certainly know the Asian group is staying in the home without the knowledge of the real estate company. Lorelee Mogg told me that the owner was not local. I cannot imagine that the owner would be renting the house without the knowledge of the real estate company. I would like to help those kids but I hesitate to bring anything into the house when they are not there. It might frighten them and it is sort of like abetting a trespass. We have to think about this matter before we do anything more."

From left: Pat Davis, Joan Savage, and Jeanne Olin

(photo by Jack Savage)

CHAPTER V

ANOTHER CHANCE

Joe was waiting for Jessie when she returned home.

"Do we have any plans this evening? I just got off the phone. I was talking to my old FBI buddy, Larry. He is in town meeting with a new agent who is working around here. He suggested that the four of us get together for dinner. I thought that if it met with your approval, we could have dinner at the Shore House on Lover's Point. We could go for a sunset dinner."

"That sounds like fun. I haven't seen Larry for ages. I am so glad you have kept in contact." Joe had been a detective in San Francisco when he first met Jessie a long time ago. He had contacts with the FBI and remained friends with some of their agents. Jessie enjoyed the relaxed friendships that still remained. It was fun to reminisce about beautiful San Francisco.

"I'll call Larry and let him know that dinner is on. I'll suggest about 5:30. Hopefully, that gives him enough time to get down here." Joe seemed anxious to see his old buddy. "I'll also make reservations for us. It should be a beautiful evening to sit out on the deck."

Jessie and Joe lived so close to Lover's Point that they could walk to the Shore House. Larry was already seated at the bar with his agent. The four were ushered out to the deck. "I would like you two to meet Brad Brennan. He is a newer member of the bureau. I've told him all about you two," Larry smiled.

Jessie was impressed by Brad's smile and warm handshake. She noted how his suntan complimented his sandy hair and blue eyes.

"Welcome to the Central Coast of California, Brad. I am sure you'll enjoy living here and I hope to see a lot of you," Jessie said enthusiastically.

Joe also welcomed Brad. "Well, Larry mentioned he told you all about us. I am glad you are still willing to have dinner with us. I am certainly anxious to hear about you. You look like someone who would enjoy the life here on the Central Coast. We have a lot to offer in the way of any sport that interests you. Do you enjoy water sports or climbing?"

Brad laughed. "I do enjoy hiking and climbing. The ocean is really my first love, though. I surf and dive and swim. I also passionately love kayaking and spying on those cute otters. Thank you for welcoming me to the Central Coast. I have considered this home for some time. I am originally from a town close to San Francisco. I went to Cal Poly and hung out a lot in Santa Cruz. Other than some time in Louisiana diving for oil companies, I've spent my life in California."

"I might have known," Jessie grinned. "You have the look of a surfer. I mean that as a big compliment. You didn't get that tan working in an office. How does that work for the FBI?"

"Actually, those are great abilities for an agent on the Coast of California," Larry cut in. "Diving and climbing and even surfing are pluses. Brad is an agent that I am very proud to have hired. He truly has a flare for adventure and, most importantly, problem solving in an area where knowledge of the ocean is a plus. He has unique qualities that make him a true asset."

"That's quite a recommendation coming from my old friend. Cal

Poly is a great school. I am sure you studied more than surfing while you were there. You couldn't have a better cheer leader than Larry. He's impressed a few people in his day and he appears to still be going strong," Joe added. "I am guessing that you two might be looking into the strange happenings regarding a diver right off shore here. I won't say any more."

Larry nodded at Joe. "Perhaps you two should order some wine. Dinner is on me. I will tell you that it is an interesting case. It is going to be common knowledge that we have been called in. I am afraid this is going to have international aspects. That is all I can tell you at this point."

Jessie ordered her merlot. "Larry, you are always good for plot ideas for my novels. Now I have the dashing, young, new agent in the picture. My imagination is soaring."

"Jessie, all I am saying is that the FBI is taking a look at the matter. We are not even sure we are needed," Larry chuckled. "Don't let her frighten you, Brad. She writes mystery novels. She solves a variety of crimes in her novels. Joe was a detective in San Francisco, so the detective or agent always gets his or her man."

"That's reassuring. I love a good mystery. I also really like being called dashing. I have never been called that before." Brad sat back and relaxed. He knew he was around friends.

"Do you have many friends from college remaining on the Coast?" Jessie asked Brad. "Is your family close by?"

"Unfortunately, most of my college friends have moved on. I have a few surfer buddies remaining. I wish I had kept contact with one person in particular, but I didn't. I am very sorry about that. My family isn't that far. They are still in Contra Costa County."

The evening was very pleasant. The sea turned bright rose outside of the deck. The air was warm and very calm. The four friends enjoyed themselves and reassured each other that they would get together soon. Jessie and Brad exchanged emails for future contact.

Walking back to Jessie and Joe's home, Jessie commented on Brad's easy going personality.

"I really don't believe in arranging dates for friends, but I wish I could do that for Brad. He seems rather lonely. I'll have to think about that."

Joe shook his head. "Brad seems like he is very capable of making friends. Let's invite him to parties and celebrations. I would not start arranging dates for him."

Jessie agreed. "Speaking of parties, I think it would be fun to have a Halloween party. We should think about that in the morning."

"And who are you going to invite for Brad?" Joe laughed.

"What do you think of Belle?"

*****

Jessie met Mary the next morning at mass. The two decided to have coffee at the Roasters to catch up with the recent events. Jessie was also anxious to talk to Mary about a Halloween party. It was very easy to convince Mary that a Halloween party would be fun.

Mary had pretty, very curly blond hair which gave her a very upbeat appearance. She had a sparkly personality and was always ready for fun.

"I think a Halloween party would be a lot of fun. I don't know if I have any costumes I could wear. Maybe John and I should wear matching costumes. I'll think of something. By the way I would like to go by that house you and Joan went to the other day. I am very curious about that group of kids. I would think we would be able to put them in touch with people that could help them. I am not sure what language they speak but I am sure we could connect them with someone that speaks their language. When we find out their language, we can call the DLI. The Defense Language Institute has teachers from all over the world. The DLI would be a great place to start. John has a friend that works there. He would help us."

"That's a wonderful idea, Mary. I hope they used the vouchers from St. Vincent de Paul for some clothes. They can stop by the churches in Pacific Grove for lunches. I will stop by the house with you." Jessie was ready.

The house seemed as deserted as it was when Joan and Jessie stopped by. The only difference was that today there was a sign that indicated "NO TRESPASSING" in big red letters. Jessie walked up onto the porch and knocked. Mary shook her head. Jessie tried the door anyway. The door was locked.

"Let's get out of here." Jessie climbed down the steps. "Mary, look over there." Jessie pointed at the small figure that had just crawled out of the house through the broken window.

Mary turned to look and the figure took off running down the street.

"Stop, I would like to talk to you!" Mary shouted. The young boy did not stop. "Well, at least he has jeans on. They must have gotten some things from St. Vincent de Paul. Doesn't LaVerne work there?"

"Yes, she does volunteer there on Mondays and that would be today. Let's walk over there and see what she knows. I think she gets there about now." Jessie and Mary were off.

*****

LaVerne was in the back room, ironing.

"Yes, they were in last week. They probably came in right after they received the vouchers. I wasn't here but I heard about their appearance. They should be coming in some time again today. Rod told them to come in today because they needed shoes. We were out of shoes when they came in but Rod told them he had them in another store and that he would have the shoes here today. He talked to the girl because she appeared to be the only one that could speak English. They are from Cambodia. They are really confused, according to Rod. He said that they appear to be very frightened but he indicated that he didn't want to pry and he didn't want to know too much. He said they appeared very respectful. He said that there were three very young men, probably teenagers, and one young girl. The box with the shoes arrived. It's over there in the corner. Rod wanted them to have first choice."

While LaVerne was talking, the front door opened and the young Cambodians entered. The young girl, Lee Hong, did the talking. She explained to the clerk that Rod had told her that he would have shoes for them. Lee handed a voucher to the clerk on which Rod had indicated that they could have any shoes that would fit. He indicated that they could also be given additional clothing.

The clerk knew nothing about the shoes and did not know where they were. "I have the shoes back here. Come on back." Laverne waved the young group to the back room. Lee noticed Jessie and stopped. Jessie waved her into the back room.

Lee looked at the shoes and was thrilled to see a hot pink pair. The young men were pleased to find a very nice collection. They pushed their feet into them and found pairs that seemed to fit.

"I am from Cambodia. Can I help you?" a lady volunteering at St. Vincent's asked the young group. She repeated her question in a dialect Jessie could not understand. Lee burst out in tears. The woman, Dora, went to the young girl and hugged her. "Don't worry, you are safe here. We will try our best to help you. Why don't we all go to my house and have some tea. We will help you if we can."

Lee looked at Dora hopefully. She looked at Jessie, Mary, and LaVerne and shook her head. "They are all right. They go to my church. They are good people. Come with me and we will have tea and cookies and you will feel better." Dora led the young girl out. Lee nodded to the young men to follow. Jessie, Mary, and LaVerne followed.

CHAPTER VI

AMAZING GRACE

Life in Cambodia is hard for most of its population. Human Rights Watch has expressed concern over proposed laws that restrict organizations that work in poverty reduction, child protection, and human rights. The government in Cambodia has been slow to act on these matters. Cambodian girls that are poor are often used as virtual sex slaves and young boys are often bought for use on ships that stay out at sea for long periods. They become a modern type of serf. Their freedom must be bought back by labor on ships on which human conditions are horrible. Vermin run throughout the ship and are everywhere. The boys are sometimes beaten and shackled and can be resold to other ships. Many of these boys are never able to buy their freedom. They are used to fish and mend nets. The fish are often sold to huge conglomerates that sell the fish to well-known pet food companies. The ships are very difficult to police because they can stay out for very long periods of time. They receive supplies from supply ships that rendezvous with them at sea. This is the background from which Lee Hong, her brother, Manny, and his two friends, Akara and Bora came.

Lee Hong sat at Dora's table drinking tea. The ladies sat at the table while the three young men who did not speak English sat on Dora's comfortable sofa, also sipping tea. Dora encouraged Lee to tell the ladies how she arrived in the United States. First, she indicated she wanted to know something of Lee's background in Cambodia. Dora assured Lee that her motive was not to inform the authorities. She indicated that she wanted to help the young people that came from her country. Dora explained that her family fell upon bad times and that they were very fortunate to have relatives in California that worked for them to be allowed to enter the United States.

Lee hesitated. Manny, her brother, spoke to her in an angry voice. She answered him softly and he returned to drinking his tea. "My brother is worried that I will tell you about our arrival in the United States and that you will have us deported. I told him that we need help and that I trust you."

Dora nodded and spoke to Manny and his friends in a low voice in a dialect that they understood. They seemed less agitated. Dora smiled at Lee. "Please continue."

Lee began her story. "My father was a writer in Phnom Penh, the capitol of Cambodia. It isn't a good idea to be a writer in Cambodia, particularly when you were a writer who cared. My father cared. He felt it was necessary for him to speak out about some of the injustices that he saw every day. He felt he needed to help the very poor. He knew that he would be putting the family in danger. He placed me with a friend of the family as a nanny. He trusted that they would see that I would be educated. I had learned English from my mother's friend. That was attractive to my father's friend. He placed my brother with another friend. He also promised to have my brother educated. Things went very wrong for my father. The government held him in disgrace. We never saw our parents again."

Lee stopped and for a moment broke into tears. It was evident she was trying to be strong. Mary put her arm around her and hugged her. Dora offered her a tissue.

"Stop for a moment, darling. I know how hard this must be for you. You are safe now. We will see to that," Dora promised.

After some time, Lee continued. "I was told by my father's friend to leave his home. My presence would be viewed as sympathy for my father. He wanted none of that. He gave me nothing. He suggested I try to find work elsewhere. I decided to try to find my brother, Manny. He had not fared much better. I went to the place I believed Manny lived. I was told he, too, was sent away. I was informed that he was told to try to find a job in tourism or the garment industry. I knew he was somewhere in the capitol.

"To my great relief, I found him. He was in the process of applying for work in tourism when he met a fine gentleman who told him he had plenty of work for him but it would involve leaving the country on a boat. Manny introduced me to Mr. Chun, who offered me work also. It was to be wonderful. Mr. Chun told us that we needed to pay him $900 for our transportation. Neither Manny nor I had any funds. Mr. Chun told us that we could work for him on the ship and pay him back. We agreed to work to earn our transportation. It seemed very simple. It wasn't simple.

"The ship was not what I expected. It was awful. I could see rats running around as soon as I boarded. We had no quarters. My brother was to help with fishing. I was to work on nets. I was to be the only woman on board, which frightened me. Mr. Chun assured me that I would be more valuable if I remained a virgin so I needn't worry. I wanted to cancel our arrangement. The workers on the ship were obviously mistreated. Then I saw a man in shackles and I knew. We were not going to be allowed to leave the ship. Mr. Chun informed me that the man had tried to escape before he had paid for his trip.

"One day became another without notice. We were hungry and tired. We felt hopeless. I wanted to die and might have attempted suicide but worried about my brother if I did. Mr. Chun would probably hold him responsible. He had made friends. Akara and Bora were also caught in Mr. Chun's web. The three seemed to watch out for me. We worked very hard so were not beaten by Mr. Chun. We kept our eyes down and any affection we showed to each other was not within his view.

"One day, another ship pulled alongside ours. We were told by other workers it was a supply ship. The supply ship would enable our ship to stay out longer. There would be no chance of a discovery being made at the dock. There would be much less chance of escapes of crew or workers like us. I became convinced that I would die on this ship.

"I noticed Mr. Chun going over to the supply ship. The conversation between Mr. Chun and the captain of the supply ship became animated. The captain started waving his arms. The crews of both ships were obviously waiting for the fists and knives to be needed. I became terrified when Mr. Chun pointed my way and at my brother and his friends. Were we to be sold to another ship? We knew the horrors of this ship. We did not know what we had to look forward to on another ship. Mr. Chun crossed back over to our ship.

"As I feared, Mr. Chun had sold us. He came over to our group of four and told us to go over to the supply ship. My protests and questions were met with a snarl and a push in the direction of the supply ship."

At this point, Lee again broke down. She was comforted by all the ladies. Manny looked very uncomfortable.

"Take your time. You are among friends." Dora patted Lee's knee.

Lee continued, "We walked across the gang plank. I thought of throwing myself into the water but again I thought of my brother. We were pushed down onto the floor and told to wait. The captain came over to us. He informed us that we would not be on his ship long. We would be transferred to another ship tomorrow. He told us not to bother anyone and we would get on the ship in good condition. He passed us some sort of gruel. We were hungry. We ate and did not talk. We waited.

"The next morning, a larger ship moved next to us. Our captain went over to the larger ship. He motioned for us to be brought over. We crossed over with no comment. The captain of the larger ship carefully looked us over. He took my face in his hands and told me to open my mouth. He looked at my teeth. I felt like an animal, a dog. He nodded to the captain of the supply ship. The supply ship captain left to return to his ship. We pulled away and set out across the sea. A crew member told us to go down into the hold. There we found other workers. I still was the only woman.

"The hold area appeared to be a little better than the hold area of the last ship. I was shown to a corner where I had some place to actually lie down. My brother talked to the young man sitting next to us. He told us that we were heading for Central America. He was told that workers were needed in South and North America. He knew nothing more."

At this point it was obvious that Lee could not go on. She placed her head in her lap and sobbed. Manny stood up and went to his sister.

"No more," he shook his head, looking at Dora. "We leave now."

Dora stood up and went to Lee.

"We understand. Please keep in mind that we want to help. We want to help you find a place to stay. The place you are staying now is not going to be available for long. You are trespassing. We want to find a place for you where you are safe and you know you are safe."

"I haven't felt safe for so long," Lee whispered. "Thank you for your kindness. I am suddenly hopeful. I trust you and I believe you will try to help."

The four Cambodians went on their way.

Dora looked at the remaining ladies and shook her head.

"What can we do? I'm almost afraid to learn more for fear we will feel compelled to tell authorities and I really don't know what would happen to these kids. I would hope they would not be deported."

Jessie nodded. "I feel the same way. I have friends with the FBI. Some of them will be at our Halloween party. Right now I can tell myself that the kids are here legally," Jessie said, looking at Mary. "Well, at least I have no knowledge of their illegal entry. I am not sure I want to know more. I do not believe that refugees that come here for safety would be deported if they would be in danger in their home country. I believe these young people would be considered refugees. They probably would be put back in the same situation that they escaped from. I know that is a very shaky story but I am sticking with it. I will not discuss them with the FBI."

Mary shook her head. "Surely, amongst the four of us and our Club members, we can solve some of these problems. We cannot put these kids in a homeless shelter, even if there was one in this area. Housing is the main concern. We can provide food and even some clothing. They need housing and some sort of jobs. Anyone that has a viable idea needs to share it. I think, for now, we must keep this quiet and within our group. My heart has gone out to these kids. They are too young to be put through this much grief. Let's see if we can come up with a charity or agency that will provide housing with few questions asked."

Jessie stood up to leave. "You know, you are all invited to my house on Halloween. Let's see what we can work out before then. I think there will be a few members of the FBI there so I would caution that this probably should not be discussed at that time."

Mary and Jessie walked together on their way to their respective homes. They decided to walk passed the house that Lee had given as her address. The "NO TRESPASSING" sign was up. The one window was still missing.

"I should have asked Lorelee Mogg, the realtor, what the owner would be asking if this goes up for sale."

"I was thinking the same thing," Mary smiled. "Why don't we stop by her office? It never hurts to have a realtor as a friend."

Lorelee was at her desk when Mary and Jessie arrived. She was most helpful.

"We estimate that it would take at least $100,000 to get this house up to code. That is just getting it up to code. It would take considerably more to turn it into the charming house it could be. Investing too much in the repairs to the home is problematic for the owner. The owner isn't sure he would get a good return for his investment. The property is located in Pacific Grove, so the property itself is worth something. It might be worth more without the house. It is his decision to make and he doesn't seem to be in any hurry to work things out."

"Thank you for the information," Jessie smiled. "I wonder if some organization might be willing to make an investment of labor for a low price. When you think about the position of the owner, he or she would have to pay to have the house demolished. I would like to think about this."

"Let me know if I can help you with anything. It is so close to downtown and right by so many facilities and churches I do not believe it would be too big a problem to have it zoned for some sort of government housing for families. The big problem there is that before any group of that type could move in, the house would have to be brought up to code."

"Thank you so much for your time." Jessie stood up. "I would like to invite you to a Halloween open house at my house this Saturday. It is from 3- to 6:00 p.m." Jessie handed Lorelee her business card with her name and address.

"I would be delighted to come. I have enjoyed meeting you both. Meeting people in the neighborhood is fun and actually good business for me. Thank you for coming in," Lorelee stood as Jessie and Mary left the office.

*****

The day had turned cloudy. Jessie and Mary hurried along Lighthouse Avenue. Jessie was pleased with the meeting with Lorelee. "I think we have some good ideas from Lorelee. Now all we need is some sort of a plan and maybe we can really help Lee and company."

Mary nodded. "Yes, but we do need a plan. We also need the backing of an organization with some money."

CHAPTER VII

TRICK OR TREAT

Halloween 2015 was a beautiful fall Saturday in Pacific Grove. Jessie thought that was very convenient for having a party. She and Joe had made some snacks and went to Costco to pick up a Halloween sheet cake and champagne. Jessie had witch napkins and ghost decorations. She had a mask but wasn't sure about a costume. There was excitement in the air. Jessie was anticipating some fun when Belle and Brad met. She was sure they would like each other. They seemed to have a lot in common. There will be quite a few people at the party so she'd have to think of a way to get them together. The party was going to be fun.

A couple of Jessie's friends were coming down from Moraga.

"Kim and Meg both said they would come. I wonder if they will wear costumes. I bet they do, and if they do, the costumes will be great. No one will be here at exactly three, Joe. It is exactly three. We have at least another half hour before guests arrive."

Jessie hadn't finished making the comment when the doorbell rang and Mickey and Augie arrived. They were dressed as convicts. The party had begun.

Belle arrived shortly after Mickey and Augie. She was wearing a tiara and a maxi dress and made a pretty princess.

"Can I help with anything? Everything looks very festive and you look cute," Belle offered.

"Belle, you look darling, very royal!" Jessie smiled broadly. "I could probably use some help with the punch. I am making a mimosa punch that only takes a moment. I wanted to wait to the last moment and it has arrived."

Belle had just entered the party when Jessie saw Brad walking up the stair with Larry and Larry's wife, Laura.

"Just a moment, Belle, here come a few people I want you to meet. I don't think you've met Laura and Larry, and this is a new friend, Brad. Everyone, I want you to meet my friend, Belle. Also, I want you all to meet Mickey and Augie. From now on I will let everyone introduce themselves."

Larry extended his had to Belle and noticed she was staring at Brad. He also noticed that Brad was staring at Belle with a look of amazement. "Have you two met before?" Larry asked.

"Yes, a long time ago. Belle, is that really you? I've been looking for you for a long time."

"I've been away. I waited for you a long time. I never heard anything from you." Belle turned from him. "Jessie, you said I could help with the mimosa punch." Her hands shook but she walked away and into the kitchen.

Jessie could see that something was wrong. She could see the hurt in Belle's eyes.

Brad followed Belle into the kitchen. "Can I open the champagne?" Not waiting for an answer, he started expertly removing the cork. "I stayed in New Orleans for the whole year. I worked for oil companies diving and then knew it was not what I wanted to do for the rest of my life. I started thinking of you and wanted to see you again. I didn't want to just call you after all that time. I went back to school and just assumed you would be there. I know that was foolish. I never intended to stay away so long. One day just led to another. I thought of you every night."

Outside the kitchen, the party was going on. Joe had opened some more champagne and was pouring drinks, anticipating that the punch would be placed out any moment. Finally, Brad carried it out. Brad took two glasses and returned to the kitchen. The food was all out so the two in the kitchen were disturbed only when a new bottle of champagne was requested. Brad would open it and bring it to Joe to pour.

The conversation in the kitchen was getting easier.

"I have learned to dive now too," Belle stated. "I always wanted to dive in the Aquarium tanks and talk to the visitors. I now do that as part of my Monterey Bay Aquarium volunteer duties. I envied your fun under the sea. To work as a diver for the Aquarium, you must reach a minimum qualification certification level of Rescue Diver and have CPR and first aid education. You also need at least 20 cold water dives."

"I'm impressed. Your work for the Aquarium is all volunteer though, is that right? Do you have a paid job, too?"

Belle laughed for the first time that day. "Yes, I work for a research institute associated with the aquarium, MBARA. I love my work, both the paid work and the volunteer work."

"Do you think the Aquarium would allow me to volunteer in some capacity? I love the aquatic world. I would like to dive and work around the octopus."

Belle smiled. "I am sure they would have a place for someone with your talents. Do you have a paying job?"

"Yes, I got a graduate degree when I got back and landed a job with the FBI. I like my work very much most of the time. There are some fine people in the Bureau. I am very fortunate that they accepted me.

I've had my moments."

Lorelee Mogg walked into the party just as Jessie was about to cut the Halloween cake. "I'm sorry I am so late. Saturday is my busiest day, as you can imagine. I was showing my client around our beautiful town. On a day like this with all the pumpkins out and the funny scarecrows in the shops, the town sells itself."

Jessie introduced Lorelee to the guests she did not know. Lorelee acknowledged past clients in the group. "I'm glad I didn't miss the cake. It looks wonderful. I think a little bubbly will complement it." Joe had brought Lorelee a glass of champagne. Mickey walked over to her and reminded her that she had been her realtor. They laughed and toasted each other.

"Thank you for steering us to this town. We were wavering between here and staying put in our home in San Francisco. I will always love San Francisco but for us at this time this is perfect. All our problems worked out with regard to the short sale. You were so helpful" Mickey said with sincerity. "Please use me as a reference whenever you like."

"That is so kind of you. I have enjoyed meeting Jessie and Mary and some of the people at this party. This is a fun Halloween," Lorelee smiled. "I think I had better run. It is almost six o'clock and I want to thank Jessie for her kind invitation."

Most of the guests were finishing their conversations and edging towards Jessie and the door. Brad and Belle began exchanging information. "May I see you next week?" Brad didn't want to waste any time.

"I am going to a conference next week. Most of my time is taken. I am not even volunteering tomorrow at the Aquarium. I would love to talk to you though. Once I start the conference, I'll know more about any free time."

At 5:55 p.m., the doorbell rang and Calvin, a neighbor, made his entrance, wearing the devil's horns and carrying a drink that looked very much like vodka.

"I heard you were having a party and I knew you would want to invite me!" He grabbed Jessie and kissed her hard on the lips. "Wow! I like those costumes. I really like that neckline, Jessie. It is really you!"

Jessie stepped back from Calvin immediately. Calvin reeked of liquor and appeared to be very drunk. "Your costume is very you, too, Calvin. I see I don't have to offer you a drink. I am glad you live close by so no driving is required for you to get home." Jessie wasn't smiling.

"Oh, honey, don't you worry your cute head over Calvin. I just got back from Indonesia. You remember, I have a place over there. The trip was fantastic. I was able to combine business with pleasure. Ah, yes, a great deal of pleasure." All eyes were on Calvin.

Larry walked slowly over to Calvin.

"What type of business are you in, Calvin? I couldn't help but overhear that you just returned from Indonesia. I understand there is a lot of budding industry there."

Calvin eyed Larry cautiously. The vodka overcame any warnings that he might have otherwise observed.

"Yeah, it's great. There is lots of fun back there. I am a food broker by trade. Spend my time bartering with the Japanese over shrimp and coffee. The job requires someone with a great deal of taste in many areas. Speaking of taste, that's really a hot one over there in the kitchen." Calvin nodded towards Belle. Do you know anything about her?"

"I know she is way too young for you and she's talking to a good friend of mine."

"What was that old saying, 'All's fair in love and war.' By the way, they don't make them too young for me." Calvin finished his drink. He put the empty glass down and picked up two glasses of champagne. He walked over to Belle and handed her a glass while nuzzling her ear. "I thought you needed this, kid."

Belle jumped back. "Excuse me, do I know you?"

Brad took Belle's glass. "I'm sorry, but we are leaving. I wouldn't have another glass if I were you." Brad placed his arm around Belle and led her to where Jessie was shaking her head. "Jessie, I can never repay you for having this party. I think, however, this would be a good time to leave. Do you need any help in getting rid of Satan over there?"

Jessie shook her head. "I think Joe and Larry can handle it. I am glad you've made a new friend."

Brad smiled. "I haven't made a new friend, but I've been reunited with an old friend."

Belle smiled, too. "Thanks for inviting me to your wonderful party. I will be seeing you soon. Brad is walking me to my car. Satan is something else!"

In the meantime, Larry and Joe had walked up to Calvin.

"Joe was just telling me that you lived around here. If you need any help getting home, we will be happy to walk with you. Also, I am very interested in your business. May I have your card?"

"Well, I think I know when the party's over. I don't need help. Here's my card. Thanks, Joe."

Calvin was on his way down the block. He didn't stop to exchange good-byes with Jessie. He had a nice strong drink waiting for him at home and a puzzle to work out tomorrow.

Jessie felt good about her party as she walked her six-pound terrier, Amber, up to Lighthouse Avenue early later that evening. They walked by Calvin's house and Jessie shivered, remembering his inappropriate behavior earlier. When they turned the corner, both Amber and Jessie were startled to see all the trick-or-treaters at the coffee shop. The baristas along the street were offering hot cider to kids in costume and many a pirate was collecting treasure.

Upon their return home Amber immediately ran out to the second floor porch. There, she challenged the squirrel that made his home in the oak tree above the porch. The squirrel rained down acorns from above. The squirrel and Amber looked at each other through the glass side railing. Jessie estimated that the squirrel had a good four pounds on Amber. Amber took her post and barked away. The squirrel ceased throwing acorns and all was peaceful except for Joe yelling at the television over a bad football call. What a great season of the year!

CHAPTER VIII

NEW BEGINNINGS

Brad walked Belle to her car in virtual silence after the party. When they got to Belle's car, he stopped. "There is so much I feel I have to make up to you. I should have kept communication flowing. I got so wrapped up in diving in the Gulf and actually did some work for the FBI at that time. I thought of you all the time and anticipated seeing you as soon as I got back to California. The date of my return kept changing. I guess I just thought you knew how much I cared. I do care. I don't want to wait a week before I see you. I very much want to make up for lost time."

"The seminar that I am going to involves aquatic trafficking. I know NOAA and several other government agencies are participating. I don't know if the FBI is invited. I want to see you soon, too. I want to see you very much."

Brad looked very thoughtful. "I am not certain that I would attend the entire conference if it is going on for a week. I actually did a little work in the Gulf involving NOAA, the National Oceanic and Atmospheric Administration. The subject is very interesting to me.

Let's talk no later than tomorrow. I will call you. I promise."

"Call me Monday. Tomorrow, I am really unavailable. Monday, I will know more about the conference. I...." Belle stopped in the middle of a sentence. She noticed Calvin walking – or staggering – by.

Calvin noticed the couple at the same moment. "You're not even taking her home. Talk about losers!" He took a look at Brad and kept walking down the street.

"There is something I really don't like about that guy. As a matter of fact, there is nothing I like about that guy." He squeezed Belle's arm. "I will call you Monday."

Belle awoke Sunday feeling a little blue. *Why did I tell him I wasn't available today? I want to see him but then he was gone for so long. I still don't understand. I need some time before I throw myself into another relationship with him. He broke my heart once. Should I give him another chance? I am not sure. Once I allow him into my life again, it will be impossible to let go of him.*

Belle lay back on her pillows. She closed her eyes and began to fall asleep. Her cell phone's chimes ended her dreamy state.

"Belle, this is Jessie from the Aquarium. I know you are not supposed to help out here today but we are really shorthanded. They needed a substitute and I obliged. I was asked to call to see if there is a chance you can help out? We are doing evacuation drills and you are so good at giving them. You know every emergency exit. Besides that, we could really use a diver for the Kelp Forest feeding."

"Actually, I need an inspiration to get up today. I think a dive in the Kelp Forest might do the trick. Give me a little time. I'm moving sort of slow. I suppose you are doing the evacuation drill at the end of the enrichment today. I can make it before nine-thirty."

"Belle, you have made my day! I will treat you to a latte after the shift." Jessie was glad Belle would help out and she could have a coffee with her later. She was curious about Belle and Brad.

Belle arrived at 9:30, in time to help lead a group through the evacuation drill. The guests watching the Kelp Forest feeding were very attentive and enjoyed watching Belle. Dolphins were spotted off the tide pool deck and pelicans flew in formation overhead. In other words, it was a typical Sunday at the Aquarium.

Belle and Jessie walked to the Monterey Plaza Hotel after their shift. It was a beautiful afternoon and they decided to sit out on the deck and watch the otters and seals play. The tourists were taking pictures and pointing out a particularly active sea gull on top of the fountain.

As they sat back and sipped their lattes, Jessie said, "This is really special. A really great morning and then a fantastic latte with a friend who I was really anxious to see." Jessie smiled. "I was so proud of myself to get you two together. I met Brad and thought that you would enjoy him. It was a surprise to see you already knew each other."

"Yes, he was the love of my life when I was in college. Then he suddenly went off to work in the Gulf of Mexico and we lost touch. I was devastated. I didn't see him again until yesterday at your party. I just don't know, Jessie. He wants to go on as if he never left and that the years between didn't exist. I told him I wasn't available today. I needed time to think about what I wanted to do. I am going to a conference this coming week and I thought I would take that week to really think about the matter. He wanted to call me today and I told him to wait until Monday. I guess I don't want to be put in a position to be hurt by him again. After all, Jessie, he just dumped me."

"It doesn't sound like he really dumped you. It sounds like he went off to work thousands of miles away and that he just thought you would be here when he came back. Remember, that was years ago and that he was years younger. You were both still in college. It was very obvious yesterday that he was thrilled to see you and that he cares for you. A student in college sometimes doesn't realize that inaction can be decisive. They can sometimes be so intent on getting things accomplished that they have tunnel vision."

"I don't know, Jessie. When we dated, he was intense but he also seemed to value the pleasure of surfing and being carefree. I thought we were in love. I know I was in love. But then, he left for a summer job and I never saw him again. I can still remember how empty I felt. I joined the Peace Corps for many reasons. I know one of them was to get away for a while. When I ran along the beach, I thought I saw him out catching waves. When I went for coffee, I would think he would come up behind me and hug me. I had to leave the area. I am not sure I can trust him."

Jessie was sympathetic. "I think you should go slowly, if you are hesitant. I also think that you can meet the right person at the wrong time. It is unusual that you meet that person again and that it is now the right time. I'm not really making any sense."

"Yes, you are. I understand what you are saying. I will sleep on it. I will see how persistent he is."

*****

Monday arrived with an autumn breeze. Belle pulled on her snug Aquarium sweatshirt and her warm Uggs. She was glad to be going to the Aquatic Trafficking Conference. She really was not responsible for anything during the conference and could enjoy just listening in the back row. The conference was to be held in one of the boardrooms of the Aquarium. Belle stopped at Starbucks for a latte on her way, and then stopped at the registration desk to register when she saw his name on the list. *I cannot believe Brad got into the conference this fast. I am not ready to talk to him.*

Brad was seated in the first row with note pad on the table in front of him. Belle slipped into the last row as planned. The speaker took his place in the front of the room as soon as Belle was seated. He began by explaining that he was an agent for the U.S. Fish and Wildlife Service, one of the leading agencies involved in aquatic and wildlife trafficking. He indicated that other agencies of the government can also become involved particularly, when the trafficking is international, which it is so often. The Coast Guard and the FBI, among other agencies, have been involved. The biggest problems for agencies involved are budget problems and lack of agents. Unfortunately, trafficking has increased.

The United States is the recipient of much of the illegal animal and aquatic trafficking. Records show that the smuggling rings have links to drug cartels in Mexico and South America.

Belle was fascinated by the speaker's information. She knew that the Aquarium had been used to hold evidence for trials involving aquatic trafficking. For the most part, the evidence was coral from protected areas. She was surprised to hear about the bladder of the endangered totoaba fish. The speaker indicated that poachers referred to the bladders as aquatic cocaine. Soup from one bladder could be sold for up to $25,000 in China. These fish are found in the Sea of Cortez. They can grow to be six feet long and can weigh as much as 200 pounds. Penalties for poaching these fish include up to 20 years in custody. The smugglers remove the bladder from the fish, leaving the rest of the carcass to rot on beaches.

The morning passed quickly for Belle. The speaker announced a short break. Sandwiches and soda were brought in. Brad spotted Belle as soon as he turned. He waved to her to get her attention. She smiled back at him as she approached the lunch table.

"I am probably not going to be attending any more days of this conference. I was told that the FBI was interested particularly in the totoaba fish, as it is smuggled to this country and often drug cartels are involved. Are you enjoying the conference?" Brad asked.

"I found it absolutely fascinating. I knew nothing of the totoaba fish. I am looking forward to going to the Sea of Cortez soon as part of my job. I am told there is a wealth of aquatic treasures there but knew nothing about that fish," Belle answered.

"I would love to go the Sea of Cortez, but I would like to go there strictly for pleasure," Brad added. "Speaking of pleasure, would you have time for a wine or coffee after the conference today?"

"No, I don't think I should do that tonight. I need to sort some things out. I need this week to myself. Meeting you again on Saturday was wonderful. It also stirred some memories that are unpleasant. I was desolate when you stopped communicating with me. I do not want to put myself in that position again."

"I understand, and I want to make it up to you. Can I call you on Saturday morning? It will have been a week from last Saturday. I won't say another thing to you today if you promise you will take my call. If you say no, I'll cause a scene right here," Brad promised with a shy smile.

Belle laughed. "How can I say no to that?"

"I'll call at eight in the morning. Get to bed early on Friday," Brad instructed. He returned to his seat and took notes the rest of the day. At the end of the conference he nodded to Belle and was off.

Belle enjoyed the rest of the conference. She also enjoyed the fact that she did not feel she needed to hurry any decisions. The week flew by and by Friday evening she felt she was in a good place.

Saturday morning at eight o'clock sharp her phone rang. "I was waiting for your call. I am ready for a great day!"

"Great, I'll pick you up in ten minutes. I have some ideas for the day. We can discuss them over breakfast. Make that fifteen. I have to pick up some lattes first."

Brad arrived at Belle's door at exactly 8:15. He greeted her with a hug. "I thought we would enjoy our lattes at the beach and then have breakfast wherever you like. Bring your wet suit in case we decide to do some snorkeling. It should be a sunny day. The clouds are moving out as we speak."

"Wonderful! I need to ease into the day. This latte is a nice way to slowly warm up." Belle slowly moved back from Brad.

The water was calm when they pulled up to Asilomar Beach. It was still overcast but the sun was doing its best to warm the morning through the clouds. Brad's car was cozy and comfortable.

"Let's just stay here for a while and enjoy our lattes. I feel warm all over," Belle said and laid her head back on the seat. "Saturday morning is so special. I refuse to schedule anything that isn't fun on a Saturday morning.

"I did a lot of thinking over the week, Brad," Belle said. "I decided I wanted to have fun. I don't need to spend each day worrying about the past or stressing over the future. I don't know where the wind will carry me. I only know that today I am warm and content. I am content sitting here next to you today, looking at the beach and the ocean."

"So often, we forget about today," Brad reflected as he sipped his latte. "Today is all we have. The past can enrich our lives and bring us sad or happy memories, but it is no more. The future may never come. We can plan, we can pray, we can study, but what we cannot do is ignore today. It was the future. It will be the past. I am content to sit next to you and share this moment in time. Your nearness makes me happy."

Brad and Belle were sitting above the tide pools that were made famous by John Steinbeck. They watched as a father and his son climbed among the rocks. The father was cautioning his son to be careful. The son was ecstatic as he held up a treasure for his father to examine.

"Look out there, Brad! I just saw a whale spouting to the right of that whale-watching boat. I noticed that the boat was just hovering over there. I thought perhaps they had spotted something."

"Oh, yes, I see it over there. Looks like a grey whale. How awesome! It's easier to spot the spouts now that the clouds have rolled out. They show up much easier against the blue sky. What's all that red stuff over there? I've not noticed it before," Brad stated.

"I think they are pelagic crabs. I heard about them at the Aquarium. They are usually found down south but, with the weather being extra warm this year, they have moved further north. They don't last long on the beach. Look at the birds flying around. They will soon have a feast. This is really neat. There is so much life to witness from the comfort of your car while sipping a latte. I am feeling very lazy. I have no desire to move right now. Brad, look over there. Isn't that the obnoxious guy from Jessie's house? I think his name was Calvin."

"You are right. I recognize him even from this distance. It looks like he is looking for something. He has a metal detector and I think he has thrown a rake on top of that towel over there. If you lose something on this beach, you really have a problem. I wonder if he is more pleasant sober. I doubt it for some reason."

As Belle and Brad watched, a playful dog off leash came running over to Calvin to sniff around his feet. Calvin angrily waved the metal detector toward the dog. The dog's owner came running over.

"Come on, Scotty. Leave the gentleman alone. He is busy." The owner snapped on the dog's leash. "I am sorry, sir. He's just a puppy."

"Get him away from me!" Calvin snarled.

Brad chuckled, "Actually, I don't think he is pleasant when he is sober. You really have to make an effort to be cross on such a morning in this beautiful place. Calvin has obviously made the effort."

The dog and his owner continued their run down the beach. Calvin continued his search along the shore, stopping to bend down and examine articles along the way and then throwing them back on the sand. Calvin did not look up toward Brad's car. Brad and Belle did not acknowledge Calvin.

After watching with interest the happenings on the beach, Brad suggested kayaking. "I am not starved at the moment and I think we might enjoy hanging out with some otters first. I can rent a kayak for us at Lover's Point and we can maneuver it down to San Carlos Beach. Then we could have breakfast in that area and do a little snorkeling. I would love to spend the day hanging out with you and some otters. What do you think?"

"You are the man with a plan. I like the idea of using a kayak as a means of transportation for the day. I could use a little sun exposure. I'm in."

Brad and Belle drove to Lover's Point, rented a kayak, and slipped into their wet suits. Brad pushed the kayak with Belle in it into the surf. The sea was calm and they slipped down the Bay hanging close to the shore. They passed the Aquarium and waved to some of its guests. Out in the Bay they passed several kayaking classes. They carefully tried to avoid otters at rest in the kelp forest. They laughed at one in particular who was making a huge racket banging a shell of some sort against a rock. He really seemed to be working hard for his lunch.

Belle and Brad pulled their kayak up onto San Carlos Beach and spent some time snorkeling nearby. They strolled to the coffee shop in the Monterey Plaza Hotel and feasted on breakfast Panini and fruit.

"I feel like I earned my breakfast. What a great display of beauty just a little under the surface of these waves. I could do nothing else but snorkel and scuba dive on that beach and I would be happy. It is really a work out though on a lazy Saturday morning," Belle sighed. "I will let you handle the kayak on the way back to Lover's Point. I am feeling like I should reserve my energy for a little more beach time there."

Belle and Brad kayaked back to Lover's Point and hung out on that beach after turning in the kayak. The afternoon merged into evening. A young couple who had been diving moved in next to them.

"Would you care to share some of our food? I am Paula and this is Preston. We have plenty to go around."

"How sweet it is of you to offer! I am Belle and this is Brad. Oh, my! You do have plenty of food!"

Paula had come over and was offering a tray loaded with fruit, cheese, and baguettes. "I have been helping out at a deli in Monterey. Half my salary is food. It suits our life style. We're very seldom hungry. Where are you two from?"

Brad stood up to accept a cheese slice and baguette. "I have a bottle of wine in the trunk of my car. Too bad we cannot have it on the beach."

"Our motor home is parked down the road. We have a view of the ocean and it would be great to have a little wine with our cheese," Preston offered.

The four nodded and Brad stopped at his car to unload belongings and pick up the wine. They strolled down the road a little and came to a small motor home. Paula carried the food into the home and placed it on a cute table in front of the window which looked at the ocean. She pulled out wine glasses and napkins while Brad poured everyone a little wine. "Where are you two from?" Brad asked. "You seem to have a little bit of a Canadian accent. That's just a guess."

"You found us out. We are from British Columbia. We are just not ready to commit to a permanent address yet," Paula sipped her wine. "We bought this mobile home and have been traveling around the coast ever since. We will probably spend most of the winter in California along the coast. I pick up jobs in delis and restaurants and Preston picks up odd jobs. He does a little construction work when we are out of money. He has experience as a house painter and can even get jobs on fishing boats. He is also a talented artist and sells his work in conjunction with other artists at farmer's markets. Would you like to see some of his art?"

"I certainly would like to see it," Belle answered.

Preston was already on his feet and moving to the back room. "I like these two. I sold a painting of a beautiful sea urchin this morning. It was barely dry when a passerby asked to purchase it. I was doing seascapes but I've gotten to really like painting these little guys. This area is so wonderful for artists. The views are awesome and the wild life is unbelievable. I'm really enjoying myself and the extra money is wonderful."

The paintings he displayed were bright and colorful. One painting was of the gorgeous view from Lover's Point and another featured a bright lavender urchin in amongst white rocks and blue sea.

Both Brad and Belle were duly impressed. Paula smiled proudly.

"Isn't he wonderful?" Someone knocked softly on the door. "I will get that. I bet that is Lee. What can I tell her?" Paula looked at Preston.

"Let me get it. I have a job for the men." Preston opened the door and invited Lee inside. "I found out about a fishing boat on the wharf that was hiring. No union fishermen want the job and as long as we tell them that we will join the union as soon as we can, I think we will get hired on. Tell your brother and his friends that they need to be here by 6:00 a.m. I will get us to the wharf. Belle and Brad, this is Lee Hong. Lee is looking for work and can clean houses, babysit, and do restaurant work. She is hoping to get into a nursing school but she has just arrived in this country. If you or any of your friends are looking for help, you can contact her through me."

"Thank you so much, Preston. I don't know what we would have done without your help." Lee left to hurry home before dark.

"Lee is looking better. She is still so thin, I worry about her," Paula said.

"She seems so sweet. Is there anything we can do to help?" Belle asked.

"Only if you know someone who could hire them," Paula answered.

"Actually, I have been working so much I could use some help cleaning once a week, if Lee would be interested. I can also ask around to see if any of my co-workers need someone. How did you meet Lee?"

"A few weeks ago, Preston and I were spending time around Big Sur. We found Lee hovered on the beach. Lee was the only one who spoke English. She was there with her brother and his two friends. She was utterly lost and terribly frightened. I am actually not certain what happened but I think the boat they were in crashed. I believe they were abandoned. Preston and I did not want to leave them. We got them food and brought them back with us."

Paula continued, "Living like we do, we have friends in the homeless community. We brought them to one of the safer encampments and allowed them to be introduced. When I went back the next day, I was told they had worked out some sort of housing. They were given information on church programs for food. I know that there are benefits for such people in Canada. I know very little about the programs in the United States. I believe there are much fewer programs. Frankly, I was afraid to find out too much. I do not want to have to notify authorities."

Preston nodded. "I put the word out that if they needed help with working, I would try to help. They got the word and we've been in touch ever since. I don't want to get them in any trouble."

Brad said very little. He had a pretty good idea what might have happened. He did not want to share his thoughts on the matter. He would look into it at another time.

Belle and Brad soon made their departure from Paula and Preston.

"I am afraid the day has finally caught up with me and that I need to get some rest," Belle said with a grateful smile. "I have had a wonderful day."

"I understand. I am a little tired myself. I will call you tomorrow."

"I am volunteering at the Aquarium tomorrow, but I would like to hear from you. What did you think about Lee Hong? That whole story seemed so unusual. She seems very lost. I would like to help if I could. I wonder what happened."

Brad didn't speak for a few moments. "I think I need to look into the matter. Lee and her friends did not just arrive on our shores by accident. I don't want to frighten them. I want to do some investigating. When do you think you might use Lee for cleaning?"

"I am not sure. Perhaps I can use her next week. I am having some friends over and the place could use a little freshening up. I just feel I would like to do something for her. I will let you know what I work out on Monday."

Brad helped Belle get her equipment into her condo and held her close. "I am so happy that I have found you again, Belle. I know I am a lucky guy, no matter what happens in the future."

CHAPTER IX

THE WEB

"Jessie, would you like to have coffee or wine after shift? I need to talk to a friend" Belle smiled as she stood by the information desk.

"That sounds like a plan. I vote for a glass of wine at Pierce. It is such a nice day; we can sit out on the patio. Joe is watching football. He won't miss me."

"That would be nice. I want a little bit of privacy."

The day was sparkling and the sky was clear. The shift went by swiftly and Belle and Jessie were at Pierce Winery at 2:00 p.m.

"I just felt like talking to you about Brad. I have made several speeches, mostly to myself, about living from day to day. I truly believe that it is important to do that. My problem is, I care too much for him. His smile, his touch, his voice, even his cologne, remind me so much of the guy I fell in love with. It is hard to forget yesterday. It is even harder to not think about the future. I try not to think about it and I certainly do not make any plans. It is just so hard."

"I understand that you were hurt by him. I know that there is a lack of trust. I think if you deny yourself the joy that today is bringing you, however, you would be allowing the past to rule the present and even the future. Give yourself some time. Tell me about your date yesterday."

"Yesterday was great! We spent the day either in the water, on the water, or by the water. We met the nicest couple who are living in a motor home on the beach. Doesn't that sound like fun? A strange thing happened though. A young Cambodian girl came over, inquiring about work. She is here with her brother and his friends. The couple found them around Big Sur. Their boat had crashed. I am going to try to use her as a cleaning lady."

"Is her name Lee Hong?" Jessie asked.

"Yes, it is. Do you know her?"

"I cannot say I actually know her. She came to St. Angela's for food when I was there. We know she is living in a vacant house in the neighborhood with her brother and his friends. She has gone to St. Vincent's for clothes. Her family was caught in a political upheaval. I believe her status here is very sketchy and I certainly know they need help. My friends and I are trying to decide what can be done. I am not sure about going to the authorities at this time, but I am sure something needs to happen. I don't want to make matters worse for them. I have done some research. If they are victims of human trafficking, they would be treated as refugees by the Office for Victims of Crime under the U.S. Department of Health and Human Services. As such, after HHS Certification, they would be eligible for federally-funded benefits. Judging from the little information that I have, I believe they are victims of human trafficking. All the evidence I have points to that conclusion. There are many unanswered questions. Lee started to tell us about her past and broke down. I have not discussed this with Joe. I know he would inform the FBI. What did Brad say?"

"He was obviously very concerned. He indicated that he would do some investigating. I have a hunch he feels the same as you do and will get the authorities involved. Perhaps you should get together with your friends and tell Joe."

"That is probably what should be done, but I don't want to frighten them and have them disappear. I'll talk to Joe tonight and get together with my friends. I think Joe will be glad that Brad is involved. He said that Larry was very high on Brad and said that Brad had a very bright future with the Bureau."

"I think I've spent too much time worrying about myself. My problems seem small compared to the problems of Lee. I will try to get in touch with Paula, the lady in the mobile home. She has a way of contacting Lee. Perhaps we should talk tomorrow."

Jessie shook her head. "You cannot take care of anyone or anything unless you take care of yourself. I will tell you that I thought you looked radiant this morning. You were positively glowing."

Belle laughed, "It is just that I had a lot of sun and exercise."

Jessie decided to walk home along the trail. She walked passed the Aquarium and avoided a couple of bicycle riders as she made her way from Monterey to Pacific Grove. She looked into the distance and saw Mary, Joan, and Pat coming towards her.

"We're going for coffee and/or hot chocolate at the hotel. Would you like to join us?" Joan asked.

"Thank you, but I have been out all day. I better see if Joe and Amber have survived without me. I think we had better call a meeting of the Strawberry Wine Club tomorrow afternoon. A few things have come up regarding Lee Hong. My friend, Belle, ran into her yesterday while she was with Brad. You met them at my party. Brad works for the FBI. I should know something by the afternoon. If not, we still need to try to figure out what should be done to help Lee."

"Shall we say about four o'clock at Juice and Java?" Joan asked. "I will email everyone not here."

"That would be great," Jessie nodded. "I will see you tomorrow."

The local news on Monday morning was full of speculation and some information with regard to the body that had been found at Lover's Point Beach. Evidence pointed to a connection between a boat that had washed up along Big Sur and the body that was discovered at the beach. The boat was known as a "panga boat." It was discovered smashed and abandoned. A small stash of marijuana was found at the scene. Panga boats are sometimes used to smuggle drugs and even people from Mexico and Central America and have been found as far north as Big Sur. The body was found in a diving suit. The authorities revealed that death resulted from a stab wound. The suit had been slashed. It was believed that the body was thrown into the water after the stabbing. According to the Monterey County Sheriff's Office, panga boats are sometimes met by vans and trucks. In this case, it is believed that this was a drug deal gone bad.

The news hit Jessie hard. All sorts of issues and fears came to the surface. Jessie called Belle as soon as she heard the news. Belle had actually let Paula know on Sunday night that she was interested in using Lee Hong as a cleaning lady and that she would like her to come over Monday afternoon. Belle only worked half a day on Monday and that would be a good time for her. Paula called Belle on Monday morning and indicated that Lee would be at Belle's at 1:30 p.m.

"I think that perhaps you should let Brad know. I know Lee did not commit a crime but I think this might be getting too big for us to handle by ourselves," Jessie said slowly.

"I have made a call to him already. I haven't heard back," Belle stated. "I agree. I don't know what is going on but I know I want to help Lee. I cannot believe she's involved with a murder or, for that matter, with drugs. She is really destitute. I hope I hear from Brad before she comes."

"Call me when you can after she arrives. I am glad I told Joe last night. I think he called Larry."

Jessie hung up the phone and shivered. She fought back a feeling of panic. Was she in over her head? The food distribution would not take place until the next Monday. She thought of going to the house where Lee and her brother were staying. She went to mass at St. Angela's and ran into Mary.

"Coffee?" she asked Mary.

"Of course," Mary replied. "I cannot wait until this afternoon to discuss the Lover's Point mystery. Did you hear about the boat the authorities believe is connected to the body found on Lover's Point?"

"Yes, and I am afraid this complicates many things. Belle told me that a couple she and Brad met on Sunday picked Lee and her brother and his friends up around Big Sur. Lee and her friends had come from a boat that had some problem. I fear there may be a connection. Let's think about this at the Roasters."

"Do you think we should go by Lee's house?" Mary asked.

"I thought about that," Jessie replied."

They had arrived at the Roasters and were sipping coffees. The weather had grown cool and there was a prediction of rain. Somehow, it suddenly felt like winter.

"I don't want to do anything that would frighten them off. I am upset. I believed we could work things out and possibly make things better for them. I don't want to go there and frighten them. I am just not sure what to do. Lee is innocent. I don't know what happened, but I cannot believe she had anything to do with murder or drugs. My feeling is that she is a victim who was innocently caught up in all of this. I think we need to wait to hear from Belle. We should know something by late afternoon. Hopefully, Brad will have gotten involved. He has met Lee. Has everyone from the Club been called?"

"Yes, we are all to meet at Juice and Java," Mary answered. "Jessie, this has gotten so confusing. I wonder if we should tell the realtor, Lorelee Mogg, about the unwanted guests in the property she is handling."

"Why would we do that?" Jessie asked.

"Because we know people are trespassing on property she is responsible for," Mary replied.

"We should probably have talked to her before, but remember, we decided we needed a plan and that we would wait until we could find someplace else for Lee to live. Now, unfortunately, I think the police might have a plan of their own." Jessie looked out of the window. It had started to rain very hard. "This is really such a beautiful place and sitting in a warm coffee shop with a warm drink is very special. Can you imagine how different it is for people that are homeless? I just pray that we can help Lee. She really touched me. I don't want to see her so frightened she moves out of that house and into the streets," Jessie was thoughtful. "I did give her address to Joe when he asked."

"We both have a lot to think about. I think I need to just wait until we get more information. Hopefully, we will get good news this afternoon by the time we meet at Juice and Java. My exercise class awaits, so I have to go. See you this afternoon."

Mary ventured out in the rain with a shiver.

Jessie checked her email before leaving the Roasters. She looked up and recognized Lorelee Mogg in line for a warm drink. Lorelee spotted Jessie at the same time. She picked up her drink and joined Jessie.

"I just wanted to thank you again for inviting me to your party. This rain is really welcome, but you were really lucky to have it so nice the day of the party. I had a great time and enjoyed your little patio so much."

"I am so glad you had an enjoyable time at the party. I am happy to have the opportunity to talk to you out of your office," Jessie smiled.

"I am just remembering that we discussed a property that our company is handling in my office. This rain is going to cause some problems with that property. There is a huge leak in the kitchen. We are going to have to move toward doing some minimum repair or more damage will result. I am going to get someone in there as soon as the rain stops. I cannot quite remember. Are you interested in the property for yourself as an investment?" Lorelee asked.

"Not really. I was actually thinking about a charitable group taking it over. Perhaps they would be able to obtain it for a very reasonable amount and perhaps they could use people who were homeless to help bring it up to code. It was just a wild thought. I am so concerned about homeless people in this area. In the summer, when there is no rain, homelessness is not the best way to live, but rain raises homelessness to a whole new level."

"That's actually an interesting idea. I don't think it is a wild thought. It might be a win-win situation. Before we even begin to think of something like that, we would have to look into the coding restrictions in that area. The area is coded for commercial use but I don't know if housing of the homeless would be accepted. In the meantime, when I get back into the office, I have to look into having repairs done so that further damage is not sustained," Lorelee waved as she went out the door.

Jesse was stunned. She knew that Lee and her brother and his friends were going to be discovered if repairs took place. She was also stunned that Lorelee Mogg did not immediately toss out her idea with respect to housing the homeless. The meeting at Juice and Java would be quite exciting.

Brad arrived at Belle's condo as she waited for Lee to arrive.

"Let's go out for a hot chocolate. Lee is not coming. I will explain and let you know what happened.

Belle was startled. "What do you mean, Lee is not coming? Paula told me Lee would be here at 1:30 p.m. What happened?"

"I told you Saturday that I would be doing some investigating. I did just that. Don't worry about Lee's safety. She is in good hands. Let's go down the block to the coffee shop. I need a strong coffee."

They walked down the block in the rain and hurried into the coffee shop. "I really don't know Lee, but something about her touched me. I really cannot believe that she would willingly do anything involving drugs or anything else. Jessie knows her and believes she may be a victim of crime."

"That's actually what our thinking is at the Bureau. Lee, her brother, and her brother's friends are in custody but are being held in a residence run by Social Services. They are all under the age of 21. The Pacific Grove Police assisted us in this matter. As soon as we got their location, we decided to move. Joe Anthony passed on their address to the FBI. The Pacific Grove Police had noticed activity around the house where they were living. They moved in immediately when they got the word from us. We have also detained Paula and Preston."

"You don't think they have anything to do with this matter, do you? They were so nice and seemed so happy." Belle shook her head and warmed her hands on the thick mug of hot chocolate.

"We really don't know yet. They might not have realized what they were getting into. The fact that they were hanging out at Big Sur at the same time this panga boat arrived is rather a big coincidence. Of course, anything can happen, but my feeling is they might have been involved in some manner. Perhaps they were to pick up drugs. I'm not sure. Maybe they are completely innocent."

"How can you just hold them when you really have no evidence? That hardly seems fair. They seem like such nice people," Belle said, annoyed.

"We could not just hold them without actual evidence. We have evidence of some minor drug dealing on their part. I think I need to stop discussing this matter at this time. I just felt it was necessary for you to know that Lee was okay. She and her friends were not safe living where they were. They were brought here to this country by someone for an illegal purpose. Perhaps they were brought here by the dead man."

"Brad, someone else is involved. You know that. I don't think Paula and Preston could have arranged an international drug deal. If this is drug trafficking and/or human trafficking Lee and her friends were really not safe."

"That's part of the reason I think we need to get back to where we left off at Lover's Point. You need to let the experts handle this and I want to have a personal relationship with you. I don't want to see you caught up in this."

"I want that poor young girl to know she has friends. I know Jessie Anthony feels that way. Lee has no one in this country. She has no family or friends in this country other than the people that have helped her from St. Angela's and Saint Vincent de Paul. They care and want to help. Please, let her know that if you can. She obviously trusted Paula and Preston. Her trust may have been misplaced. I hope not. I want to help her if I can. I don't want her to feel the whole world has let her down."

"I understand and I will see to it that she knows she has friends in Pacific Grove." Brad took Belle's hand. "I love you, Belle. I know you want to take things day-by-day and I respect that. I just want you to know that I am not going anywhere this time without keeping in touch with you. I have to get back to work. I will call you tomorrow."

"That would be fine." Belle didn't move. "I am staying here for a moment."

After Brad left, Belle just sat by the window and watched the rain. It was peaceful and beautiful in its own way. She was concerned about her relationship with Brad moving too fast. This afternoon had been very hectic. She walked out into the rain and into her condo. She sunk into her favorite chair and called Jessie.

"At least I am thinking about someone other than myself this afternoon, Jessie. I cannot get Lee out of my mind. I also feel really strange about Paula and Preston. They were so sweet to us and we got them arrested."

"Belle, you did not get Paula and Preston arrested. They got themselves arrested if they in fact were involved in drug trafficking or in human trafficking. I think Lee is in a safer place than staying in the abandoned house. It was only a matter of time before she and her brother would have been discovered. The realtor told me this morning that she was going to have the roof repaired before more damage occurred. I am sure the trespass would have been discovered at that time. As much fun as I think crime-solving is, I think we need to concentrate on helping Lee. She certainly is a victim."

"You are right. Let me know what the Strawberry Wine Club comes up with," Belle said.

The Strawberry Wine Club arrived at Juice and Java one by one. Jessie arrived first and started to push tables together in an alcove in hopes of some limited privacy. Mary came in next and started helping with the tables.

"You look particularly fashionable today in that new top. It looks so cute with your blonde hair," Jessie commented. The ladies of the Strawberry Wine Club had many adventures but always took care to look fashionable doing it.

Joan, Pat, and LaVerne arrived next. They were followed by Mickey and Lettie. Lettie had just arrived back in Pacific Grove from her summer in Toronto.

As the ladies filtered in, each went to the counter to order a beverage. Most ordered red or white wine. Those were the choices of fine wine at Juice and Java, plus a few coffees or even a glass of water.

"I think this is all of us that are coming today," Jessie spoke first. "We are glad to have you with us, Lettie. We missed you over the summer. I think all of you know that a couple of us have been concerned about a young Asian girl, her brother, and friends. If you have been watching the local news you have heard that there has been a break through with regard to the body found at Lover's Point a few weeks ago. A boat was found washed up around Big Sur. It is a panga boat. Panga boats have been linked to drug smuggling in the past. The authorities believe that boat is tied into the apparent murder of the person who washed up at Lover's Point. Authorities also believe that the Asian girl, her brother, and friends were on that boat. At this time, the members of the group are considered victims of crime. There have been other arrests. I can tell you that those of us that heard Lee Hong's story believe in her innocence."

"I was one of those that heard Lee's story. I cannot imagine that she was not telling the truth. I just have no idea how we can help," Mary added. "I would really like to assist her in some manner. That being said, I have no idea what we can do. I thought there might have been a chance we could help with housing, but now that does not seem to be an option."

"Where have the authorities placed these kids? If they are being treated as victims, surely, they are not incarcerated," LaVerne jumped into the conversation.

"I think I can find out where they are. I was told that Social Services is assisting in this matter, as they are very young. I would hope they are all together. They must feel isolated and so alone. I know very little about this type of law but I would be pretty sure that they would have the right to have an attorney appointed on their behalf. We should be able to find out who that is. We certainly can offer assistance helping them. We do have some accumulated expertize in this group."

"We could perhaps offer to transport them to various educational programs and help with various appointments," Mickey added.

"I heard that the kids are Cambodian. If that is true, I have a few Cambodian friends who might be able to help. My friends have been in this country for some time but they might still understand the background of this group. They also might be able to make certain resources available to them," Lettie volunteered.

"I think we have some good ideas and if and when the murder investigation is complete we might be able to give considerable assistance to Lee and friends. While it is going on I think we should consider the property they used for shelter. I think the address is 14 Amber Street. I talked to Lorelee Mogg about it this morning at the Roasters. She came in out of the rain after you left, Mary. She asked me if I was still interested in it. That was when she told me she was about to have it repaired when the rain stopped and I started to panic. I told her that I had an idea regarding the purchase of the house by a charitable group. I mentioned that my thought was that they would be able to purchase it at a very reasonable price. Then I hoped that perhaps the clients they served might be able to work on it and bring it up to code. The house would then be used for housing the clients. I told her I thought it could be a win, win situation," Jessie stopped to take a breath.

"Did she give you the impression that she thought you had lost your mind?" Mickey asked.

"Not really. She actually said she didn't think it was such a wild idea. She was going to look into coding laws in the area. We would have to keep the coding in mind when we try to find a charitable group that would take it on. I have a couple of ideas with respect to the groups it might work for. I thought of a charity that might provide housing for kids that age out of foster homes. I also thought it might be used by low income vets who come home with no place to live and a desire to attend a college or junior college. It could also be perfect for a charity that wants to provide housing for young women who are in need of some help. Of course, there are many other charities that can use housing of this type," Jessie said, looking at the rest of the club.

Mickey seemed very interested. "Augie is a member of a men's charitable group. They raise a lot of money for their charity. I can talk to him and his group about the thoughts of our group. They might be interested in taking this on. I am sure it would have to be a charity that needed minimum supervision. They would want nothing to do with supervision. They would only be interested in providing some funding."

Jessie was pleased. "I will talk more to Lorelee Mogg. Hopefully, there is nothing in the coding laws that would prevent a low profile charity to take this property over. I originally thought about this property for Lee Hong and friends. I am not sure but I think that if they are considered victims of crime their housing wouldn't be their main problem. Let's see what happens in the next few days and we can get together again soon."

Jessie and Joan went to the real estate office of Lorelee Mogg the next morning. Lorelee motioned for them to come to her desk. Jessie smiled, "I was just wondering if you had the chance to look into the coding laws that cover the house at 14 Amber Street."

"I actually was going to call you later in the day. That area is coded for business and residential use. According to that coding it would be all right. Then, of course, the neighbors might have some input. As you know, Pacific Grove moves very slowly on these matters. Recovering addicts or felons could certainly not be housed there without going to the courts. I am sure even the businesses in the area would have objections. Approval would be very dependent on the charitable use. The owner is a very generous person. The property in its present condition would be hard to sell. It is not in an area that is particularly sought after. The owner will consider any reasonable offer. All the mandatory reports would be done," Lorelee was a very good sales person.

Joan was rather puzzled. "How would we proceed? Would the charitable group make an offer first to the owner and wait for reports and acceptance of the offer, and then would the City of Pacific Grove have to give its approval and run it by the neighbors?"

"I know this is not at all clear. It is very dependent on the charitable group that takes over the property. When you come up with the buyer and the intended use of the property, I will approach the owner and see what he would accept for the property. At the same time, I would pass it by the Planning Commission. If there is to be architectural changes of a major nature, I would also contact the Architectural Review Board. Let's take it one step at a time." Lorelee smiled.

"Thank you for your time. We appreciate your help. If we can work something out, we will be back to discuss this matter further," Jesse and Joan left the office.

"We need to have something concrete in mind before we come back," Joan stated. "Hopefully, we'll have some positive news from Mickey."

"Joan, let's walk by the property once more before we go our separate ways. It's only a couple blocks out of our way. I think it would help to give us some ideas. I cannot remember if it had a back yard of any size." Jessie was upbeat.

"That's a good idea," Joan answered. "You mentioned that you did not think the Amber Street property would be used by Lee and her friends. I actually think it would be perfect for them if we could focus on a sort of transitional residence for kids that age out of foster care. Lee would be about the same age as the other young adults. They would be receiving some help from Victims of Crime and would be able to contribute to costs. The kids that age out of foster care would probably be getting some money for scholarships and could contribute. With someone giving them instructions they could all probably contribute to working on the house.

"I think that's a fantastic idea. Can you pass that by Mickey? She would have a concrete suggestion to pass by Augie and his fund raising group."

Jessie and Joan stopped as they approached the house. They both spotted Calvin looking around the side of the house where there was a broken window. He was looking through the window, brushing some of the cob webs from the frame of the window. "Interested in the property, Calvin?" Jessie asked.

Calvin jumped back from the window. "Well, good morning, ladies. I am startled to see you two here. What brings you to this area? There are no coffee shops on this street."

"Jessie asked you first, Calvin," Joan stated. "This is an interesting property but the normal way of looking at property is to go to a realtor. You cannot see that much through that window. Of course, you could use it as an entrance. Is that why you were cleaning off the window frame?"

"You two are being a little too curious this morning. I didn't know a realtor was involved and I wanted to take a look. Do you have a problem with that?"

Jessie laughed. "Of course, we do not have a problem with you peeking through the window, Calvin. I just thought it was rather strange. By the way, there is a sign on the door from the Lorelee Mogg agency. They are handling this property."

"I didn't notice the realtor's sign," Calvin said as he walked up to Joan and Jessie. He frowned at Jessie. "I thought your husband was the retired detective. I would leave the spying to experts if I were you. I might walk over to the realtor's office now. I will see you both around the neighborhood." Calvin walked off in the opposite direction of Lorelee Mogg's office.

Joan shook her head. "I didn't enjoy his company when he was drunk. I don't enjoy his company any more when he is sober. He is so unpleasant. It is one thing for us to break into this property, it is another thing for Calvin to break into this property," Joan laughed.

Jessie nodded in agreement.

CHAPTER X

CHALLENGES!

LaVerne received a call from the Law Offices of Zeffra Brewer, on Friday morning. "I have been appointed as attorney for Lee Hong. Do you recognize her name?"

"Yes, I believe she and her friends came into St. Vincent de Paul Thrift Store. I volunteer there a few days a week."

"Lee Hong is very new to the country and has very few friends. She mentioned that she met with you and several ladies after a visit to the store. My offices are in Monterey. I would appreciate it if I could meet with you and the other ladies who met with Lee. I would like our meeting to take place on Monday morning at ten o'clock. Would you contact the other ladies and call me this afternoon to give me their names and verify who can make that appointment? I can certainly change the time if this time is impossible for anyone. This is an urgent matter so your cooperation is very much appreciated."

"I understand the urgency. I will try to contact everyone who met with Lee. I will do anything I can to assist you. I hope Lee is comfortable."

LaVerne wasted no time contacting the Strawberry Wine Club members who had attended the meeting at Dora's with Lee Hong. She called Mary, Jessie, and Dora. The ladies were all very busy but cleared their calendars so that they could attend the meeting with the attorney, Zeffra Brewer.

St. Angela's was holding the first pizza dinner of the season that evening. It coincided with Pacific Grove's First Friday event. On the first Friday of each month, certain galleries and shops close to Lighthouse Avenue stay open late. Many of the shops provide treats, and wine is also available. The Strawberry Wine Club liked to attend the pizza dinner and then venture out to the galleries. Most members of the club were in attendance and there was some discussion of the meeting with Lee's attorney, Zeffra Brewer.

"I am very happy that Zeffra Brewer was appointed to represent Lee. She was praised by many of my legal colleagues. She is thorough and will work hard to obtain the best result possible for Lee," Jessie said enthusiastically. "I am looking forward to meeting with her on Monday morning. Hopefully, we will get some ideas with regard to helping her."

"Not to change the subject, and I know this is all-you-can-eat pizza night, but after two pieces, I think I am ready for the galleries," Joe announced, having just finished off his dessert.

"I am ready also," Mary added. "I want to see the artist featured at the Center. I am also feeling a need for a walk."

Daylight savings time had just ended. The evening was quite dark. The pizza diners hurried up to Lighthouse Avenue where tiny lights sparkled in the trees lining the street. Jessie and Joe stopped in a small gallery just off Lighthouse Avenue. Joe had previously bought some paintings for Jessie there. The evening had become cool and the warmth of the room felt cozy. Mellow music from a young man playing a piano filled the night air.

"Isn't this nice, Joe? They have small pizza snacks too," Jessie laughed.

"Well, hello, Calvin. I didn't see you over there," Joe greeted Calvin. "I thought you said you were going out of town this week. I am surprised to see you here."

"My trip to Asia was cancelled. I have some things I need to take care of here. When did I tell you I was going on a trip?"

"Remember, we talked when you first arrived at our party on Halloween," Joe answered. "I notice you seem interested in the coral pieces. They are quite unusual."

"Yes. Well, I think I'll be moving on. I think I'll have a glass of wine at the Center," Calvin said, starting for the door.

Jessie smiled, "We might see you over there." She was talking to Calvin as he walked out the door. He did not acknowledge her comment. "Before we go there, Joe, Lettie told me that Juice and Java was open late tonight serving both coffee and wine. They are featuring a new artist. Lettie told me he paints using very vibrant colors. Let's stop over there before we go to the Center."

Jessie and Joe ambled through a few shops before arriving at Juice and Java. They ran into numerous friends along the way. Joan was at Juice and Java when Jessie and Joe arrived.

"Isn't his work fun to look at.?" Joan asked. "His work just makes me feel happy. It is so bright and really unusual."

"I like his work, too," Jessie answered. "It is fun to look at. I think I would like to have a glass of wine here and call it a night. It is getting chilly out and I am rather tired. I really like the music here, too. This is a nice way to spend a Friday evening."

Calvin entered through the back door. He spotted Jessie and Joe. "Are you two following me?"

"Calvin, have you noticed that we were here ahead of you?" Joe commented. "Please, come in and have a glass of wine with us."

Calvin shook his head. "Thank you for asking, but I had better get home." He left through the back door the same as he had entered.

"Jessie, turn around slowly and look out the front door," Joan whispered. "I think it's him!"

Jessie slowly turned to see the man from the Butterfly Parade. Once again, he glared at her. He swiftly looked around the shop, then turned and went out the front door. Jessie could see that he hovered around the entrance talking on his cell phone.

"Who on earth is he?" Jessie asked. "Why does he look at me like that? I don't think I have ever seen him before the day of the Butterfly Parade."

Joe looked around the room. "Who are you talking about? All I see here are friends and great paintings. I have your wine here. I need to get off my feet. It's been a great evening but I think I am ready for home tonight and football tomorrow."

"None of my teams are any good this year. I think Mickey and I will go to the auction they are having in the morning across the street. I am bound to see something that I don't need. Thank you for the wine, honey."

*****

Saturday morning arrived with the sound of acorns falling from the oak tree outside Jessie's window. Mickey woke to sunshine filtering through the shades. Both Mickey and Jessie hurried their morning rituals in order to meet with LaVerne for coffee at the Roasters and then headed over to the auction in time to place silent bids on fun things in the basement and still make it in time to be seated with bid cards in hand at the opening of the auction.

Mickey was able to place bids on several items in the basement that she wanted for her daughter's shop. Jessie and LaVerne did not bid on the basement items. The three were seated at the beginning of the traditional auction. "I want to see what that Paris painting will go for. I would go up to $150." LaVerne sat with her card.

The auctioneer began with some very unusual Asian artifacts. He opened the bidding at $750 on the first piece. The Club members were surprised when a bidding war resulted. The piece sold for $5,550. Jessie turned to see the lucky winner. The Butterfly Parade man sat down, smugly smiling to himself.

"I want to get out of here. I am uncomfortable. Call me if you get the Paris painting." Jessie left the auction and headed home. She felt eyes glaring at her as she left. She hurried across the street to the safety of her home. She was glad Joe was there watching football.

*****

Saturday morning sneaked up on Belle but then arrived with a ringing of her phone. She fumbled for her cell that she had placed next to her bed.

"Get up sleepy head. It's a great morning for us to head south on Highway 1 towards Big Sur. I thought we could look for elephant seals and have lunch at Nepenthe," Brad spoke energetically.

"I think that sounds wonderful. Give me about 30 minutes."

Belle flew out of bed to get ready. After a quick shower, she pulled on a blue aquarium sweatshirt that highlighted her eyes and pulled back her long blonde hair. She was ready for some fun. She had stayed away from Brad after Monday. They had both been busy and she knew he wouldn't discuss an ongoing case with her. Jessie had told her about the meeting with Lee's attorney Zeffra Brewer. She was curious about Brad's choice of Big Sur. She knew the boat that was connected to the murder washed up near Big Sur.

Brad arrived promptly in 30 minutes. "You look absolutely stunning. I missed you," Brad said as he gave Belle a hug.

"This was just an impossible week but I have the whole day," Belle smiled. "I do have a commitment for a night event at the Aquarium, but if I am back by 6, I am okay."

"Bring a warm jacket. You might not need it, but it can get chilly on the beach, as you know. Whales have been spotted in the area. It should be a fun day. I've picked up some soy lattes. I thought we would head to see the elephant seals first. They are out in numbers on the beach at Piedras Blancas, north of San Simeon. Then I thought we could do a little beachcombing and stop for lunch while we are heading north. I also picked up some pumpkin maple scones to go with the lattes so we won't starve."

Belle laughed. "Starving is not a concern, but fitting into my jeans is! Once again, you are the man with the plan. Let's hit the road."

*****

The late autumn day was crystal clear. The views along Highway 1 heading south were breathtaking.

"I am fascinated with elephant seals. Isn't it a little early for them to be hanging out? I thought they usually hit these beaches in December."

"That's true. They are a few weeks early this year. I wanted to take a few pictures. I know the perfect turnoff for picture taking. The views around the Piedras Blancas Light Station are fantastic. I am not sure of the schedule of the Light Station but we might be lucky enough to get in," Brad continued.

The seals were cooperative and almost seemed to pose for their pictures. The bizarre animals are in this area to give birth and nurse their young. The females can weigh as much as 1,600 pounds. The males can weigh as much as 5,000 pounds. Brad and Belle hiked along the beach and ended up close to the Light Station. They decided against taking a tour of the station. They did not want to rush the day. Every moment together was precious.

Looking at the cliffs and headlands, it was easy to understand why ships throughout history had difficulty sailing these waters in rough weather. As Brad and Belle walked along, they stopped to admire the expansive views. "The wreckage of the boat involved in the murder was found not far from here," Brad stated.

"I'm curious as to where Paula and Preston fit in to the story. I cannot see them taking their motor home right up to the beach," Belle said.

Brad shook his head. "Actually, there are RV campgrounds all around. We think a van was also involved. We believe that Paula and Preston are very frightened and would like to be cooperative. I definitely think they were in over their heads in this matter. If they testify in a timely manner, they will probably receive two tickets back to Canada. We would let the Canadians do what they want with them. They've overstayed their welcome in this country."

Belle and Brad headed for Nepenthe and lunch. They were not disappointed. The restaurant is located in an unbelievable area high up on cliffs above the sea. There are restaurants on various levels. The views are stunning. Brad and Belle wandered through the various areas. They stopped at the Phoenix Shop where Belle purchased abalone earrings for a friend. They stopped at a table along a railing overlooking a cliff to order a light lunch.

"Try a glass of this chardonnay. I think you will like it. As I am the designated driver, I'll pass and have one of these great sparkling lemonades," Brad said. "I won't even have one wine when I am driving on this part of Highway 1."

"This isn't a restaurant; this is an experience. I have been here once before but it was raining. It was absolutely lovely in the rain but it is just awesome on a sunny day. I am so impressed," Belle smiled. "Thank you for bringing me here."

"It is my pleasure. I want to take you to Julia Pfeiffer Burns State Park. It is not far from here and is just beautiful with a spectacular waterfall. Unfortunately, once again the day is flying by. We'll do it another day very soon. If we are to get you back by six, we have to get started. I know you are working at the Aquarium tomorrow, but we'll figure something out for next week."

Brad continued seriously, "I do not like to bring you to your home. I want to bring you to my home. I should say I want to bring you to our home. I know what you are going to say. You want to take it slow. That is very hard when you are in all my dreams."

"I do need to take it slow, Brad. I have had a magical day today.

Let's enjoy the beautiful drive home."

Brad took Belle's hand. "I understand. I can wait. I will wait."

*****

Rain was predicted on Sunday but Jessie felt it would come very late. The sun was out when she started her walk to the Monterey Bay Aquarium. She left Joe sleeping and slipped by Amber who had been walked and fed. The bike trail that she walked along to the Aquarium was roped off for another race taking place on the trail. Jessie made the detours that were necessary, looking forward to seeing her shift partner Nancy at the information desk. Nancy had been in Italy for over a month on a wonderful vacation. Jessie really enjoyed working with Nancy and was anxious to hear about her adventures. She was also anxious to see Belle and hear about her adventures.

Jessie stopped to take a picture of the silver Monterey Bay when she saw them. The Butterfly Parade man was puffing away on a cigarette talking in an animated fashion to Calvin! Jessie quickly decided not to take a picture and hurried by them. They were not looking her way and she hoped they did not see her. She did not glance back. She hoped the large tree behind them hid her from their view. What an unlikely couple.

The volunteer lounge was packed with the Sunday 1A shift. Nancy was sitting right in the front and had saved Jessie a seat. Jessie checked in and sat down next to her. They both hugged.

"I cannot wait to see your pictures! Nancy, you look fantastic," Jessie said as she sat down next to her partner. Jessie waived at Belle, who sat at the next table.

The enrichment began and everyone ended their conversations.

Nancy had many interesting and funny comments about her trip to Italy. In return, Jessie told her all about the murder mystery occurring in Pacific Grove. She kept thinking about Calvin and the Butterfly Parade man. She made a mental note to tell Joan about seeing the two together. She thought she would mention it to Belle, too, but only Joan appreciated Jessie's fear of the Butterfly Parade man.

Nancy, Belle, and Jessie decided to go out for a hot chocolate after their shift. Nancy was exhausted and hadn't gotten used to the time change. Belle was exhausted because she had a busy Saturday and then worked at a night event at the Aquarium. Jessie was just anxious.

"Jessie, I have never met the Butterfly Parade man but if he hangs with Calvin and smokes he has two strikes against him already," Belle said as she was getting up to leave the coffee shop. "You be careful and let me know how it goes in the meeting tomorrow afternoon with Zeffra Brewer."

Both Nancy and Jessie also got up to leave. Before she left, Nancy said, "My advice to you, Belle, is to have fun with Brad. He sounds like a real winner."

Jessie waved to both her friends as she started back down the trail. The race was over and she was happy to see that no one she knew was present and there were no more detours.

Monday morning found Jessie sitting at the 8:00 a.m. mass at St. Angela's. No one she knew was in the church so she planned to walk home without stopping for coffee after the service. Communion had been served and she sat back in her pew. She felt the person behind her very close. He was kneeling and his head was practically on her shoulder. She tried to move away.

"Stop your snooping around, lady. Mind your own business or you'll regret it."

Jessie was startled. By the time she turned around the man had slipped out the door. She could not see his face. She felt his walk was that of the Butterfly Parade man but she wasn't sure. She stayed for the end of the mass and exited the church. She looked down the street and saw no one. A very strange week had begun.

Jessie mentioned her experience to Joe. It was quite frightening and yet with her appointment at Zeffra Brewer's office she didn't take the time to worry about it. She knew Joe would pass the information on to

Larry. Joe also told her to mention the incident to Zeffra Brewer.

The appointment started on time. Zeffra Brewer was very professional.

"I know you have had limited exposure to my client, Lee Hong. The authorities have decided they will not press charges against my client. They are certainly treating her as a victim of crime. They believe she was brought to this country with the plan to use her as a sex slave. I know she confided some of her story to you. She knows no one else in this country to the best of my knowledge other than people we believe might be involved in some manner with the incident. Anything you can add to her story would be appreciated."

Jessie was very troubled. "I must tell you I received a threat this morning while I attended mass. I do not know if there is any connection but I fear there might be." Jessie explained what had happened that morning.

"I understand from the FBI that you have some close friends with the Bureau. If you touched upon anything that is or could be incriminating, I can understand how it would cause discomfort to someone having committed a crime."

"Jessie, your friend Calvin is a little suspicious. Joan told me that he was peeking through the window at the house on Amber Street."

Zeffra Brewer looked particularly interested. "Are you talking about the house that Lee and her friends lived in? Is Calvin a person that was at your party?"

Jessie looked stunned. "How do you know about Calvin and my party?"

"I have friends in the FBI, too. I don't often have a client that so many people seem to want to help. When did this peeking incident occur?"

"It occurred after Lee was taken into custody. Joan and I were walking by the property when we saw him peeking through the window. We knew that Lee had lived there and have talked about the property for a possible charitable use. He seemed rather upset that we saw him at that time," Jessie answered.

Zeffra Brewer was very interested. "I'm appointed to represent Lee Hong. I am trying to see that she can remain in this country, if she wants to remain. At this time, with no contacts back in Cambodia, that appears to be her best option. I believe getting this murder investigation out of the way will also help her cause. As long as there is any suspicion of guilt, we cannot really move on getting her settled. I represent only Lee in this matter. Her friends are represented by other attorneys in the event there is a conflict of interest. I am in close contact with the FBI. I would be careful in any interactions you have with Calvin. Report anyone that threatens you in any way. I will report your threat at church this morning. I think it is more likely than not it is connected to this murder."

"Can you tell us anything more with respect to how Lee ended up at Big Sur?" Mary wanted some answers before they left the attorney's office. "Lee was still back in Asia when she stopped her story to us. It seems so unlikely that a boat from Asia would just come to Big Sur."

"I don't believe it did," Zeffra Brewer answered thoughtfully. "Lee and her friends were transferred to another boat. She had been spotted, I am guessing, by someone on the supply boat that visited the original boat she and her brother shipped out on. I am not completely sure of the facts because, of course, Lee doesn't exactly know what happened. I am sure that she and her brother were brought to Puntarenas, Costa Rica. I think the intention of the boat owners was to use her in the sex industry. She is exotic and beautiful so she would bring a very good price. Her brothers and his friends probably would be used for several things. I am sure something else was on the boat that was to be smuggled into South or North America. Perhaps some Asian art that needed to be smuggled out of the country. For some reason, they were shipped north. I believe they made a stop around the Sea of Cortez to pick up some cargo. Some problem arose on their way north between the captain and crew and the boat ended up on the beach around Big Sur. That is a very sketchy summary."

Mary seemed puzzled. "Why did you ask to see us? We would like to help Lee and feel she could benefit from some of our connections with available food and clothing, but we certainly know very little about the case and do not speak her language. Excuse me, Dora speaks her language. How can we help you?"

"I knew that at least a couple of you had met with Lee and that you also had been in contact with Calvin. He is a person of interest for several reasons which I cannot disclose. I also thought I would arrange for you to meet with Lee for tea. I could arrange the meeting for some time later in the week. I believe she is in danger so I do not want her going out. I would arrange for the meeting here in my offices and I would have her brought here. If nothing else, I think she would enjoy seeing someone that was kind to her in the past."

Jessie looked at her friends. "I think I can speak for all of us. We will be happy to help Lee and will keep you informed of anything we might discover on our own."

*****

Calvin sat on his porch Tuesday morning, smoking a cigarette and watching who walked past. Jessie walked by on her way to 8:00 a.m. mass. He was seldom up this early and he noticed that Jessie was somewhat surprised to see him.

"Good morning, Jessie Anthony! How are you on this lovely morning? You're looking very sporty in your high boots."

"Thank you, Calvin, I am happy to see you up in such good spirits this morning."

"Are you going to mass, as usual? Then off to coffee with one of your friends?"

"I'm amazed at what you know about me. Yes, to both of your questions."

"You would be amazed at how much I know about you! I have read your books. I also see you when you don't see me. I hope you have a very relaxing day. Watch your step." Calvin paused. "I mean, these old sidewalks are rather uneven and I wouldn't want you to trip and fall."

Jessie continued on her way to St. Angela's. *Should I consider that a warning or am I getting overly sensitive? Why would he be considered a person of interest?*

Calvin settled back down on his chair and put out his cigarette.

I find that woman very annoying. She and her retired detective husband and his friends in the FBI. I would like to see them taken care of along with some of her so called Strawberry Wine Club members that are so snoopy. I've stopped by some times at Juice and Java when they were in the midst of a "Club Meeting." They have always laughed and acted like they were having a good time. I dislike them intensely. I was brought up Christian. I do not hate people but I may dislike them intensely. If something tragic happened to them, I would not shed a tear.

The FBI told me not to leave the area without notifying them. What do they have on me? So I do business with Asian individuals and have had a few close calls in regard to business transactions. That's absolutely no reason to make me a person of interest in a murder. I didn't commit a murder. Fred did that. I certainly wouldn't have knifed the guy. What good did that do? He keeps a low profile and I get all the attention from the Bureau. I don't know if we'll ever get to sell the stuff, and the girl is probably lost.

*****

After mass, Jessie met with Joan and Mary at the Roasters.

"I think he is just trying to make you uncomfortable. He has been named a personal of interest by the FBI, so I think we had better give him some distance," Joan said, sipping her orange juice. "The person I cannot get out of my mind is the Butterfly Parade guy. I wish we could find out something about him. If Calvin is a person of interest, so is that guy. The fact that you saw him talking to Calvin is enough for me to believe they are up to no good. I wish we could find out his name or somehow get a picture of him. I know that sounds ridiculous, but I bet he has some sort of record. What I cannot figure out is why he seemed to zero in on you."

"I cannot imagine when our paths ever crossed. I really think he was the man that threatened me at St. Angela's yesterday. He never speaks to me when he has seen me. I…" Jessie stopped midsentence. "He's standing by the door talking on his cell phone again."

Joan and Mary turned to see him. "That is him, Jessie. I'm going up there and tell him he is smoking too close to the door and it is bothering me. Come with me and maybe we can find something out about him and what his relationship is with you."

Joan was out of her seat before Jessie could protest. Jessie followed close behind.

"Excuse me, sir, but your smoking is annoying to us. Could you please move away from the door?" Joan did not hesitate.

Taking courage from Joan, Jessie blurted out, "Why have you glared at me whenever you have been close to me? Have we met before? Have I offended you in some way? I certainly do not recognize you."

"Well, I recognized you, lady. You are Jessie Anthony. You've posted your signing party invitations on the bulletin boards in several coffee shops. I recognized your name. Let's just say, I know you and your husband from your reputations. You tend to annoy me." He stepped on his cigarette, glared at both Joan and Jessie, and stomped away.

Joan and Jessie looked at each other as they returned to their drinks.

"I am sorry, Jessie. I don't think I helped the matter."

"Yes, you did, Joan. I got a picture of the jerk on my cell phone," Mary gleamed, smiling. "I just sat in my seat, he wasn't paying any attention, and I took the picture. Let's see how it turned out. Look at this!"

Mary couldn't contain herself. It was a perfect picture of the Butterfly Parade man. It was a side view but his features were clearly visible.

"We need to send it to the authorities. I think if we email it to Zeffra Brewer she will get it to the authorities and perhaps show it to Lee. Email it to me, too. I want to show it to Joe. He might recognize the guy from the past. I certainly do not recognize him. He does seem to know me, though. I am so glad you got his picture, Mary. Referring to him as the Butterfly Parade man is getting old."

Mary sent the email picture to Zeffra Brewer and to Jessie. Joe did not recognize him from the picture. "Obviously, he could have changed through the years, but I don't recognize him at all. Let's forward the picture to Larry. Hopefully, it will ring a bell with someone at the Bureau."

It wasn't until Friday that Zeffra Brewer called Jessie. "I have set up the meeting for you ladies with Lee on Tuesday afternoon. If it works out, I would like the same people to meet at my office at three. We will have tea and talk."

"Did you show the picture to Lee? We were hoping to have had identification from somebody. We have not heard from the Bureau. Neither Joe nor I recognize him. He does seem to know us," Jessie sounded disappointed.

"I have not shown the photo to Lee. I wanted to hear from the Bureau first. I will probably show Lee the picture before you arrive if the Bureau agrees. I don't want her to be influenced by anyone, not even you ladies. The Bureau has not notified me of any reason to keep the photo from Lee. I am looking forward to seeing you and your friends at three on Tuesday."

*****

The picture was making the rounds in the Bureau. Brad had a copy with him when he picked up Belle on Saturday morning. It was raining and Brad had picked up a couple of lattes to have in the car. They had seen each other during the week on very casual dates. They took walks on the trails around Asilomar, Carmel, and Point Lobos. They talked and laughed and enjoyed themselves. They had planned on a picnic on

Saturday but were very happy to be visited by the rain. California was in the middle of a drought. They could change their plans.

"I loved waking up to the sound of the rain this morning. I laid there for a little while, just enjoying the sound and warmth of my covers. Then I remembered our date and I couldn't wait to go out and enjoy the day." Belle smiled.

"I couldn't wait to see you. The rain is great but you are my sun." Brad sat back and looked at the silvery sea in front of them. "Look, I think I see a pod of dolphins over there. It looks like a lot of them."

"I see them. They actually look like a dark streak on the horizon but when I look through your binoculars I can see them just jumping. Wait until I tell Jessie and Nancy. They'll envy me. It is so much fun to watch."

"I was going to ask you if Jessie sent you the picture of the man she calls the Butterfly Parade man?" Brad asked.

"No, she did not. She has talked about him many times. How on earth did she get his picture?"

"I'll let her tell you about that. I think one of her friends took the picture. I have a copy. I was just wondering if there was a chance you have seen him. I have his picture here. We're running identification searches." Brad showed Belle the picture.

Belle looked at the picture and grimaced. "I think I have seen him. I know I thought he was very unpleasant looking. I am sure he was smoking. I just do not remember where I could have seen him."

"Well, if you remember, call me right away. He seems to have some history with Joe and Jessie Anthony. Neither one recognizes him but he identified them. We have additional checking to do. If he has gotten into any problem with the law any place, we will identify him."

"I'll see Jessie tomorrow at the Aquarium and talk more about him. It really bothers me that I cannot place where I've seen him."

*****

The Butterfly Parade man had found the forced encounter with Jessie Anthony and her friend Joan very unpleasant. He knew he tended to frighten Jessie with his scowls. He liked that he could frighten her. He did not like to be actually spoken to by that woman.

Why would she recognize me? She barely noticed me on the ship that we took through the Panama Canal. I noticed them, Jessie and Joe Anthony. Because of them, I lost millions. I was lucky that I wasn't arrested by the FBI. I had the privilege of being arrested when I returned to Costa Rica. Now, I have another chance and I am not going to allow them to mess me up again. I cannot believe they are here! It would be my pleasure to hurt them. She had the nerve to confront me and complain about my looking at her. I'll do more than look at her.

She of all people had to get involved with the girl. I thought I had Lee hidden away. Calvin wanted her first. I could have gotten a lot for her. First, Calvin could have had her. I would have gotten a pretty penny from him. Then I would have had her. I would then have put her on the open market in time for the Super Bowl in February. She is young and pretty. I could have used her for some time. She would have been fun and earned a lot of money for me. Let's face it! I saved her from starvation. Bringing her here was an act of charity. Now they have her and I cannot use her. I'll make the Anthonys pay. They will pay for interfering here and on the ship. I will not let them mess me up. I just hope Calvin doesn't get drunk and mess me up.

CHAPTER XI

SOME LIGHT

Jessie hurried along the bike trail to the Aquarium for her Sunday morning shift. The sun was bright above even though there was a forecast of rain. Jessie tried to avoid runners as the Big Sur Half Marathon had arrived in Pacific Grove. She brought along the picture of the Butterfly Parade man to show to both Belle and Nancy. The enrichment session that Sunday involved going into the Aquarium before its opening and studying the schooling (grouping) of fish in the Open Sea Section. Nancy and Jessie wandered away at the conclusion of the enrichment and were very impressed by the Japanese day octopus.

"Let's take pictures of him and show them to guests." Nancy was her usual enthusiastic self.

"I think I have a good one here. This reminds me, I have a picture on my phone I want to show you," Jessie remembered. She and Nancy hurried to the information desk to be there by the opening of the Aquarium. "Mary took a picture of the Butterfly Parade man I told you about."

The guests were just arriving as Jessie and Nancy took their posts. The clouds had moved in above the great tide pool.

"Look at that sky! I think a rainy day is the perfect time to visit the Aquarium." Belle had stopped by the information desk to say hello.

"Let us show you our pictures of the Japanese day octopus," Jessie greeted her friend. "I also have another picture I want you both to see. I have a picture of the Butterfly Parade man."

"Brad showed me the picture of the Butterfly Parade man. I know I've seen him, but I cannot remember where that was. He looks so familiar."

Nancy took a look at the picture of the infamous man. She looked puzzled.

"He is so unpleasant looking. He does look familiar. I have a feeling I saw him in a very different setting, maybe wearing a uniform." She shook her head. "I just don't know."

The rains moved in and large puddles grew in the Great Tide Pool. Very wet guests began to stream into the Aquarium, shaking off the rain from their coats and hats. The small puddles that were left were quickly mopped up by staff anxious to avoid accidents. A small child ran up to Nancy.

"Hello, Mrs. O! What are you doing here?"

Nancy laughed. "I volunteer here, Lucy. How is school going for you this year?"

"It is not the same without you Mrs. O. They said you retired. I miss you."

"I miss you, too, Lucy. You keep up the good work. I will stop by to visit someday soon," Nancy said affectionately.

Nancy looked at Jessie. "Let me see the picture of that man again. I think I remember where I saw him."

Jessie brought up the picture on her phone. Nancy looked at it again.

"It's Fred. When I saw Lucy, I remembered. He worked at the school as a custodian several years back. He was always getting into trouble for smoking too close to the school. He was not very popular with the children or the staff. As I recall, he left about three years ago. I am not sure what happened but I think he went to live in Central America. I am sure there must be records at the school that could be made available for local or federal authorities. I don't know his last name. I just called him Fred."

"Thank you so much, Nancy. I think finally we are making some progress. I am meeting Joe for lunch after shift. I will let him know. He'll take it from there and notify his FBI friends. Would you give me the school information to pass on to authorities?"

"Of course, I will help in any way I can. I am glad Lucy stopped by to jog my memory."

*****

Jessie hurried to First Awakenings to meet with Joe. The rain was falling hard as she ran into the building.

"I have interesting news," Jessie said as she moved into the booth. "Nancy knew the Butterfly Parade man. I think we can call him Fred now instead of the Butterfly Parade man."

"I will call Larry tomorrow. That's progress."

Monday afternoon brought Mary, Dora, LaVerne, and Jessie to Zeffra Brewer's office on time. Ms. Brewer asked that the ladies wait in the waiting room for a few moments. She explained she was in need of additional time with Lee alone before they would meet for tea. Thirty minutes later, she invited the ladies into the conference where Lee sat, visibly upset. She looked up with tear stained checks.

"I am happy you have come to visit with me," Lee's voice was shaky. "I hope you are still my friends. I feel so alone." She burst into tears again.

"We are still your friends, Lee. I am sorry to see you so sad," Mary answered for everyone.

Ms. Brewer brought in tea and some small pastries.

"Lee recognized the picture of the Butterfly Parade man. He briefly appeared on the ship in Central America. She also thinks he came on the ship in California before everything broke loose. She is very frightened that he is close by."

Lee spoke, "He is a very bad man. I am sure of that. He was always screaming, pushing people. I saw him with a knife. He pushed me. I am afraid he will find me and hurt me. I am very afraid. He slapped the captain. I had thought he went back. We got away. Then we found Paula and Preston. They were by the road. They said they would take us away. They offered us a ride. We had to get away. People were nice to us. Paula and Preston took us to the house we stayed in later. Now, I am here and I don't see my brother or my friends. I am lost!" Lee started to cry again.

Ms. Brewer put her hand on Lee's hand. "You are safe Lee. I promise that I will not let that man hurt you anymore."

Jessie spoke. "I think we might be close to identifying the Butterfly Parade man. A friend recognized his picture. She seemed pretty sure he was someone she knew."

"I will notify the authorities regarding Lee's identification of the man," Zeffra Brewer stated. "I think we had better end this meeting early. Ms. Anthony, I would caution you to be very careful after this identification. It appears this man is not only rude and a bully but that he is violent. I would like to plan on a meeting again in a week. We can plan on the same time and the same place. I hope we know more before then." Ms. Brewer walked the ladies to the door.

Paula and Preston maintained that they were just a young couple in the wrong place at the wrong time. They were from Canada and did come to the United States for a little sun and a little adventure. They were involved a bit in the drug culture in Canada and made a few connections in Oregon and California. Drugs were easily available and they felt that trading a little bit of them was no big deal. They met up with Calvin on the beach around Lover's Point. He helped them with trading a few drugs. They felt they were hurting no one and living very well. Preston sold some art and Paula got a job at a local deli. Life was good, they thought. Then Calvin asked them to pick up some drugs around Big Sur. They could earn quite a bit of money and decided that it made sense to do that and hopefully they would not have to resort to drug trading for some time after the transaction.

*****

Calvin had told them the approximate time of the arrival of the drugs. They were to wait by the road. They would be contacted. The night was warm and the windows in the van were down. They heard some commotion but were not concerned. They realized that this sort of transaction sometimes could run late. They waited quite some time before they realized that something must have gone wrong. Then they heard a commotion coming up the cliff. About ten men and a woman noisily arrived by the van. One of the men who could speak English told Preston that there would be no drugs or contraband coming. The woman was hysterical.

"Take her and them out of here. Take them to where you have met up with Calvin in Pacific Grove. We're getting out of here. You do the same."

Preston let Lee and her friends into the van. He said he knew nothing about how they got to Big Sur. He knew that he had to get out of the area. He drove to Pacific Grove near the homeless encampment where Calvin hung out. He took them to a deserted house close by. He told Lee and her friends they would be safe there. He dropped them off. He would not see them until Calvin sent them over to find temporary work. That was his story and he was sticking to it.

Preston was adamant that he had no idea that Lee and her friends were victims of human trafficking. He said he could not believe that Calvin would be into human trafficking. He worked with Calvin only with the trafficking of drugs. He felt he was harming no one.

Paula's story was very similar to the story of Preston. She said she was terrified throughout the night. She admitted that she and Preston were high on drugs. They were both mellow when they heard the commotion on the beach. They had messed around selling and using drugs but they certainly did not realize they were dealing with an international cartel. Money was not important to her.

"We just want to live on the land and be happy. We would never want to hurt anyone. Preston and I just want to follow the sun. We tried to help Lee and her friends get jobs. We have done nothing wrong, unless you count trading drugs as doing something wrong. If you let us go we will go back to Canada. I will be a chef and Preston will pursue his art." That was her story and she was sticking to it.

The authorities looked at the stories of Preston and Paula. They compared their stories with that of Lee's version of the night. The stories were not in conflict, but there were so many gaps.

The ladies of the Strawberry Wine Club drifted to their homes after the meeting at Zeffra Brewer's office. Jessie, in particular, was apprehensive.

"I cannot believe that Joan and I confronted a possible murderer. Mary, that picture you took was so important. Now that Lee identified the picture and Nancy, my shift partner, recognized him as a former employee of the school she worked in, I would imagine he will be in custody soon."

"I am concerned about you, Jessie. I know you'll tell Joe right away, but be extra careful. We really cannot guess what the authorities will do." Mary was very concerned.

"I will be careful. I feel we are making real progress with regard to The Butterfly Parade man, better known as Fred. Lee's story regarding him is upsetting but at least the authorities will be informed. Tomorrow, I'll get in touch with Mickey and see if Augie's group has come up with any ideas regarding the property on Amber Street. Would you like to come along with me to Lorelee Mogg's office? She was going to look into the coding of that neighborhood. I would like something positive to come out of all of this." Jessie was on her way home.

Brad looked hard at the picture of Fred. It was only a profile. He had not seen him in years and yet there was a resemblance. He really hadn't looked at it so carefully before Lee had made the connection. But now, he wondered.

It was several years ago when Brad had left Cal Poly for a summer job in New Orleans. He left his budding romance with Belle, packed his bags, and was not to return to California for over a year. He worked diving for abalone and got on with an oil company. Brad stood out because of his diving skills and his easy going manner. His hair was a little long, his tan was dark, and he was proud to be known as a California surfer. He loved to go out on the town occasionally and loved the French Quarter and Pat O'Brien's. Dixie Land jazz grew on him and he knew the summer would pass by in an enjoyable fashion.

As a college-age kid, he was approached fairly often by drug dealers. He was also approached by ladies who were "in business." One evening in particular, as he walked down Basin Street, a young lady approached him. She spoke little English. In her broken English and broken French she told him that she was from Haiti.

"My uncle brought me here. He said I would not go hungry. I was very hungry in Haiti. I am not hungry here." Brad was appalled. He gave the young girl $20 and told her he didn't need her to come to his hotel room. He said he wanted her to come with him to the police. He told her that they would help her.

"No. My uncle told me they will put me in prison and would never help me." She turned to run but she ran right into a police officer.

"What's going on here? Isn't she a little young for you, buddy?" The officer held unto the Haitian girl and slipped cuffs on Brad. "Let's go. We're really close to the station."

Brad did have a chance to protest as he was being pulled down the street. At the station, he was put into a cell. He asked for an attorney. A public defender appeared, who advised, "Don't answer anything without me being present."

"I am not guilty. I gave her a $20 and told her I wanted to bring her to the police. She started to run away and the officer was right there.

She is probably about 13. I wouldn't take advantage of a poor kid."

The public defender shook his head. "I am not sure that you are going to be believed. The fine isn't too bad. She is really a kid. Let me talk to the DA."

Brad spent the night in jail. In the morning, the cell doors were opened and he was called into an office.

"You have been checked out. The girl verified your story. She is a victim of human trafficking. You probably guessed that. You are free to go but an officer here would like to talk to you."

The police officer left the office. An agent of the FBI entered. He extended his hand to Brad. "We'd like to offer you a job. You'll have to cut yourself off from your friends and family. I will see to it that your immediate family is informed that you are alive at the present time but that you cannot contact them. They will be asked to indicate that you are working in the Gulf Area and leave it at that. It is for the safety of your friends and family that we have these rules. We believe you are the perfect candidate for a position we have open. Are you willing to work undercover for the FBI?"

Brad was stunned. He was also very flattered and excited. "I have a girlfriend that I care a great deal about."

"You cannot tell her. She and you would be in danger. It would be best if you never tell her if she waits and is willing to see you again."

Brad hesitated, "Do I have to decide now?"

"Yes. There is a problem with drug trafficking and human trafficking. You will be a very valuable asset to the bureau as you are new to the area and have very few connections here."

"How do you know so much about me?"

"We know. We need your answer."

"Is the Haitian girl going to be all right?"

"Social services will work with her. She will probably be moved out of town. She was lucky. She would probably be dead before the end of the year had you and the police not intervened." The FBI agent stared at Brad.

"I feel so much for that poor girl. No one should be in that position at 13. I am not sure why I am the person that you want but I will work for the FBI undercover for a short period of time. Then I want to go back to California."

Thus began Brad's year-long contract with the FBI. All his talents were used in an arduous campaign against human trafficking and drug trafficking. He came in contact with "Fred" when he assisted the cartel in movement of drugs within the borders of Louisiana and Texas. He was the young college kid that fit in with the college element. He also fit in with the oil industry to some extent and was able to find information on the captains of the trafficking movement. He understood that "Fred" came from California. He understood from the FBI when he was leaving his undercover role that Fred had made tracks for Costa Rica. He also understood that he was arrested in San Jose, Costa Rica.

Brad returned to college and was rehired by the FBI as an agent. He had no desire to work undercover at the present time or in the future. He was glad for the opportunity to have helped but he desired a reunion with Belle and a life involving friends and family.

I wonder if we crossed paths in California. I have had to stare at his picture to recognize him. It has been quite some time since we last saw each other. I was a long-hair college kid and was younger looking. I wore shorts constantly. Now, unfortunately, unless I am off-duty, I wear a business suit. We shall probably meet again but I want as few people to know that I was undercover as possible. I know it could be dangerous for me and the people I care about. It could really be dangerous for undercover agents still in the field in Louisiana and Texas.

*****

Jessie returned home and told Joe everything about Lee's reaction to seeing Fred's picture.

"Until Fred is arrested or out of the picture in some other way, we have to be very careful. I will call Larry right away. I am not sure they will arrest him right away. Remember, the authorities did not arrest Calvin. We know a little but there are huge gaps. There is no proof that Fred or the 'Butterfly Parade' man actually killed the person that floated up on Lover's Point. Lee said she saw Fred with a knife but there could have been other knives. Crew members ran off and no drugs or contraband was found. They will probably list him as a person of interest and keep an eye on him. It depends on what they get when they run his record. I am sure he has a record someplace. Trust me, Larry will get someone on him in any event," Joe was reassuring.

Jessie got on her iPad and emailed the Strawberry Wine Club members:

"We need to have a meeting at J&J tomorrow afternoon. We should talk about this mystery, the house on Amber Street, and most of all, Mary's birthday. Joe told me that we need to be extra careful right now, particularly because Fred might not be immediately arrested. I wish he were. Let's have a nice celebration. I will wait until after our meeting before I contact Lorelee Mogg. I am not sure if we are all still interested in trying to do something charitable with the house. I frankly think if we can raise some money we should make it happen. I am open to all ideas and thoughts."

*****

The day flew by. All the members of the Strawberry Wine Club were very busy. A few of them met at the Roasters after mass on Tuesday morning. All had fun solving the daily puzzle and talking about the wonderful rain that came down over the night. Only in California is there such a celebration over rain. Everyone was talking about the lightning and thunder, very unusual in California.

"I need to go to class," Mary said as she got up to go.

"I have to go home and type like mad. I want to do 2,000 words on my novel," Jessie said. "See you all this afternoon."

The afternoon brought the bright sun with it. Mary was celebrating her birthday that week and the arguments ensued as to who would buy her a glass of wine. Everyone wanted to do so. Mickey was wearing her signature straw hat. She looked particularly happy as she informed the Club that she believed Augie's group had come up with a plan to fund the use of the house by a charitable group for a few years. It was hoped that the charity would then be in a position to take on more of the responsibility for supporting itself.

"I have documents that Augie and his group have put together, showing how they would like to proceed. He would like Jessie and Mary to work out the initial paperwork with Lorelee Mogg," Mickey said, energized.

"Mickey, that is just awesome. We will meet with Lorelee Mogg Thursday morning. I believe her offices are closed tomorrow in honor of Veterans Day, and I work at the Aquarium. I would probably not encourage a visit, as we are expecting big crowds. Do we have anymore thoughts regarding the use we see for the house?" Jessie asked. "I see from these documents that Augie's group trusts us to decide. That is really wonderful of them. I hope the owner of the property will be satisfied with our offer. I have only talked to Lorelee Mogg. I know the owner is from out of town. I also trust that the coding will allow us to make a charitable use of the house."

Joan spoke up. "I have always thought that the house would be a perfect transition residence for kids aging out of foster care. Drugs, alcohol, and tobacco would be definitely off limits. We have to see what Lorelee Mogg has found out, but I believe that coding would be kind to a use such as that."

"I agree with Joan," Mickey added. "I know we discussed this in the past and I believe it was the most popular use suggested. Shall we take a vote?"

Everyone assented to Joan's suggestion for a possible charitable use of the house.

*****

Veteran's Day morning was a celebration on its own. The Bay looked beautiful with tiny whitecaps on the blue water. The bright sun tried its best to warm the breezy fall day. Jessie enjoyed the additional guests who filled the Aquarium. Belle had volunteered to work the shift at the request of the Aquarium staff. She would be the diver in the Kelp Forest feeding. "Any arrests that you know of?" she asked Jessie.

"Not that I know of," Jessie answered. "Larry said they were keeping an eye on me. Let's have coffee on break."

Break couldn't have come soon enough for Jessie. She wanted to talk to Belle. They found a corner table out of the way of other guests.

"I still cannot remember where I have seen Fred but he seems so familiar," Belle said as she gazed out the window of the Aquarium restaurant.

"Well, I have no recollections of knowing him and yet he certainly appears to know me. I don't know if the authorities have tracked him down yet. Has Brad said anything more to you?"

"No, as a matter of fact he mentioned that unless I had some new information to report, he would prefer to talk about more positive matters."

"He's trying to keep you out of any possible danger. That is the way the FBI or detectives in general handle matters like this. I know they mean well, but it is really annoying. I always really want to know what is going on."

"I do know that Brad was not happy that I seemed to recognize Fred. He did tell me that his picture will be passed around to Paula and Preston. You said that you saw him with Calvin, right?"

"Yes, I don't think they saw me, but I cannot be sure. I always got along with Calvin until lately. Frankly, I didn't think he had any problems with me or with Joe. I did not notice him drinking so much until fairly recently either. Actually, it was at the Halloween party that he really appeared angry for the first time. Fred, on the other hand, when confronted, indicated his disdain for me. I certainly had the impression that he knew me from the past. Their connection is hard to understand."

"Well, maybe you and I need to focus on happier thoughts. I have to tell you I am falling head over heels in love with Brad. He is attentive, thoughtful, protective, and very romantic. Besides all of that, he is so handsome. He still has that athletic surfer look about him. I am so glad that I dropped my guard. The last few weeks are the happiest of my life. Our romance was wonderful when we were in college. It is even better now," Belle glowed. "I have got to get back and get ready to dive into the tank."

CHAPTER XII

EASY DOES IT

Brad had not seen Paula or Preston since the arrest. He decided to be there when they were questioned about the picture of Fred. The Bureau had several pictures that they showed Paula and Preston. Among those shown were pictures of Calvin, Fred, Lee, Manny, Akara, and Bora. The Bureau also showed them pictures of Jessie, Mary, LaVerne, and Dora. The pictures were shown separately to Paula and Preston.

Preston quickly identified Calvin, Lee, Manny, Akara, and Bora. The agents were quite surprised when he identified Dora! He did not seem to recognize Fred, nor Jessie, Mary, or LaVerne.

Paula identified the same individuals as did Preston. She did not identify Manny, Akara, and Bora. She, too, identified Dora.

Neither Preston nor Paula identified Fred. Brad shook his head.

"Did you come upon my girlfriend and me by accident on the beach at Lover's Point?" Brad asked.

Brad was not surprised to hear their meeting was anything but accidental.

"It was kind of spur-of-the-moment, though. You two were on the beach for a while. I had met up with Calvin and he noticed you two kayaking by the shore. He mentioned that he had an interest in you two. I am not sure what that interest was. I noticed you on the beach later and I thought it might be a good idea to get to know you. Both Paula and I wanted to get out of any dealings with Calvin but I thought getting to find out some things about you wouldn't hurt and it might help."

Brad was very curious about any connection with Dora. "How do you know this woman? Did she accompany Lee?"

Preston hesitated. "We've known her as long as we've known Calvin. She has always been there. I really only dealt with Calvin but he often stopped to talk to her. She would just seem to appear. I would even say he appeared to be conferring with her at times."

"Did they arrive and leave together?" Brad asked.

Preston seemed confused. "No, I think she just came by. I had no direct conversation with her. I really am not sure but I think they just went their separate ways."

"Did she ever come to your mobile home with Lee?" Brad asked.

Preston shook his head. "No, I don't think she has ever come to the house. When are we going to get out of here? We declined having an attorney appointed. We just want to get back to Canada. We messed with some drugs. We probably wouldn't even be here if we weren't mellow that night in Big Sur. I want an attorney appointed for myself and Paula now. I am a Canadian citizen."

The questioning stopped. Arrangements were made for legal representation.

Brad was concerned. He knew that Dora had been meeting with Zeffra Brewer. He was absolutely positive that Jessie Anthony was not involved in drugs trafficking and guessed that none of the other ladies had anything to do with any illegal business.

He felt like somehow if Dora was involved in drug trafficking, she hid it completely from the other women that met with Zeffra Brewer.

It did not take a long time for the FBI working with the DEA to locate Dora and bring her in for questioning. She immediately requested an attorney. She refused to talk to anyone until her attorney was present.

Dora's attorney arrived quickly. He indicated he had been employed by her family in the past. He demanded that she be released as soon as possible. His client should not have to answer any questions while the DEA and FBI bungled along.

A search warrant has obtained to search her home. In Dora's bedroom, nothing of interest was found except for a beautiful Asian statue. Out of an abundance of caution, the agency photographed the statue. The guest bedroom was much more interesting. It was apparent that a male was occupying the room, although no one was present. The ash trays were filled to the top with cigarettes. The closet also contained at least 50 bales of marijuana.

Dora was formally arrested. The bail hearing was delayed until the impact of this new evidence was evaluated. Dora's attorney protested.

In the meantime, Jessie and Mary were unaware of the arrest of Dora when they called upon Lorelee Mogg. Lorelee had been checking the coding restrictions that applied to 14 Amber Street. She had told Mary and Jessie that the charity chosen was important.

"We are contemplating using the housing as a transitional home for former foster care kids. Is there anything in the coding laws that would restrict us? I know you would have to pass this by the Planning Commission. We have documents from the group that is funding this project for the time being," Jessie advised as she handed the papers to Lorelee Mogg. "Would you make a copy of the papers if you were taking them to the owner for consideration?"

"Of course, I will. The owner is not local. It may take a little time. I will set up a meeting with the Planning Commission in advance. I am sure I will be finished getting the owner's approval before any meeting with the Planning Commission will happen."

Jessie picked up the copies that Lorelee had made. "Thank you. You have always been very helpful."

As Mary and Jessie started walking towards their homes, they passed St. Vincent de Paul. LaVerne was in the front of the store and waved for them to come in. "I am going to be off in five minutes. I want to talk to you both."

"I need a latte," Mary said. "Let's meet at Juice and Java."

"Agreed," LaVerne answered.

True to her word, LaVerne arrived at Juice and Java a short time later. She sat down with her coffee and took a big breath.

"They've arrested Dora."

"Dora! Why would the arrest her? What did they arrest her for?"

"I don't know much, but she was supposed to be at St. Vincent de Paul this morning. Her neighbor stopped by and said they noticed police and saw her being escorted out by officers. No one knows what to make of this. She volunteers at St. Vincent de Paul. Everyone likes her. She seemed so sweet with Lee."

Mary looked confused. "She comes with us to Zeffra Brewer's office. She has heard all sorts of confidential information. I think she was the first person Lee wanted to see. She listened to Lee's story with us. Maybe she really wasn't arrested. If she was arrested, she might have been arrested for something completely unrelated. Yet, officers usually do not escort you to your car for a parking ticket."

Jessie agreed. "This just doesn't make sense. I cannot believe she could have been involved with drugs. She is so nice."

"Dora's neighbor said that she was shouting and was very angry. I have worked with her. I have never seen her shout. I hope this is some huge mistake," LaVerne said, clearly upset.

"I'll ask Joe to ask Larry and Belle to ask Brad. Hopefully, they will shed some light on this, although they sometimes will not talk."

Jessie looked at her cell phone as she was receiving a call. She could see that it was from the office of Zeffra Brewer. She immediately answered it.

"Ms. Brewer wanted me to tell you that your next meeting in her office has been canceled," the receptionist advised. "Please inform your friends. She will let you know when she might like you all to visit with Ms. Hong again."

Jessie took a deep breath. "I have a feeling that her arrest is connected to Lee Hong. I am not sure, but we may be all suspects. I will call a meeting here this afternoon at four o'clock. I am going to ask Joe to find out anything that Larry will tell him and also call Belle. Please do any checking that you can."

Jessie was happy to see Joe at home. She began to tell her story to him.

"I don't think Larry is going to pass on any confidential information to us at this time," Joe said. "The FBI doesn't do that. I will call him to make sure that you are in no way a suspect in this matter. I am sure you are not. He will tell me that much."

While Joe was calling Larry, Jessie called Belle and told her what was going on.

"Jessie, I will call Brad now. He has been really quiet on this matter. I would imagine he will tell me that you are not a suspect. I am sure if Dora was really arrested because of the Lee Hong situation he will not want to talk about that matter, either."

*****

Dora sat in a room at the sheriff's office. She was angry and fearful.

"You have been identified by two people. Drugs were found in your house. Do you want to plead no contest? If we can keep the charges to possession of drugs and dealing, you would probably never serve more than two years. If we try to work out a deal you might not get any time," Dora's attorney spoke in a low voice.

Dora looked at him. "I am innocent. I want no deal. I am being framed by the police and by people who are trying to make their own deal. I want to plead not guilty."

"Drugs were found in your residence. Are you saying you do not know how the drugs got there?"

"I know of no drugs in my home. The police or some drug dealer must have put it there. I am innocent!" Dora started to sob.

"The police have said that a male was obviously living in your house. He was in the room with the closet full of drugs. Who is he? The police have been watching your residence since you were arrested. No one has entered your home."

"He probably knows you have arrested me. He is a family friend. He knew my husband. I am allowing him to stay in my home for a short time. When can I go home?"

"I will try to have bail set. It is difficult. In the past, smugglers pay bail then skip out of the country. Authorities are becoming hesitant to set bail."

"I own my home. I have lived in this country for years. I am not going to flee. I want to sue. People will think I am a criminal. They will want nothing to do with me." Once again, Dora burst into tears.

"I will do my best to represent you. You need to participate in your case and try to help. I will be back tomorrow."

"No, wait, please! I cannot stay here! I am frightened. I did not want to help them. They have control over my family. They control everything. I had no choice."

Dora began her story. Her attorney listened intently. By the time she finished it was quite late.

"We will have to wait until tomorrow morning. I am going to try to make sure you are made comfortable. I am hoping you will be released soon. I will do my best and I am a very capable attorney."

*****

Belle was able to reach Brad. He said he could not talk about the case. He did not believe that Jessie was a suspect. He did not believe that any of Jessie's friends were considered suspects, with the exception of Dora.

Larry's message was very similar. Jessie was definitely not a suspect.

That afternoon, the ladies of the Strawberry Wine Club met at Juice and Java as planned. The mood around the table was much less festive than usual.

"I feel so bad. I cannot understand how I could have misjudged Dora to this extent. I feel somehow used. I really thought she was a very kind person," LaVerne complained, still upset.

"We were all misled," Mary said thoughtfully. "Then again, I cannot but wonder why we all just have jumped to the conclusion that Dora is guilty of a huge crime. I feel disillusioned but I don't want to be too fast to judge. She certainly doesn't fit the image of a drug trafficker as far as I am concerned."

"I am just happy that none of us are considered suspects," Joan sighed. "Thank you, Jessie, for looking into that. I also feel that we shouldn't be too quick to condemn Dora. There is always time for that when more evidence is in."

"I agree with everything that has been said. I am worried and hope that nothing that we've done will hurt Lee. I do not believe that Dora was allowed to see Lee other than at Zeffra Brewer's office. I know Lee seemed to be so happy to find someone that could speak her native language," Jessie commented. "I hope this doesn't cause her more pain. She has definitely suffered enough."

"Have you heard anything about the Butterfly Parade man, Fred?" Joan wanted to know.

Jessie shook her head. "No, I have not heard about any arrest. Fortunately, I have not seen him, either. My suggestion is that we all try to keep up on these events. I would also like to suggest that we start talking about Thanksgiving and happy events. I cannot believe how quickly the holidays have crept up on us. This morning, I noticed that Lighthouse Avenue has put up their Christmas wreaths. We haven't even had Thanksgiving yet. I think that this is almost too soon. We just started making Thanksgiving plans. I think Joe and I are going to Asilomar."

"John and I are going, too," Mary spoke up.

"Can I join you?" LaVerne asked.

"Norma and Kathy are due back in Pacific Grove before Thanksgiving. We'll have to find out if they want to join us," Mary added.

"That was fast. Now we can move on to the Christmas party," Jessie laughed. "I also have a brilliant idea. I think we should plan a couple days trip in February to the Apple Farm. We have a bunch of birthdays in February. I think it would be a fun way to start the year."

"This is more like the Strawberry Wine Club I know and love," Mary added. "We would be back in time to plan the Mardi Gras party!"

*****

Dora had a restless night. She worried that she would never get her life back. She had been happy in Pacific Grove. She had forgotten how horrible her life had been before she came to this country. She was cold in the room provided to her. She had not brought anything from home. The bed was cold and the blanket was thin. She slept for a short time and woke to a soft rain outside her window. Since she moved to California rain in the early morning had always made her feel snug and comfortable. Now, it made her wonder if she would soon be out in the dampness on cold nights. She shivered as she remembered.

Her life as a child was full of fun and happiness. She felt safe and loved by her family. Then one of the many political uprisings in her country changed everything. He came to her house and searched it with his gang of thugs. She tried to hide but he found her. She was beautiful. He thought she looked at him with fear and yet with hope. He decided to be a hero.

"Come with me. I will protect you from the other soldiers. I am their superior. Your family will be spared."

Dora felt she had no choice. He could certainly take her even if she refused. She knew her family could be slaughtered with a wave of his hand. If she went with him, it would at least postpone the inevitable. She looked at him and lowered her eyes.

"I will go with you as you ask. Please, spare my family."

*****

Dora would soon find out that the man she went with was General Amara Chun. He had much success in the political faction that had taken control of her district. She was told she was lucky by the women in the camp where she was to live. He was schooled and had a certain belief in honor. He knew Dora had never been with another man. He actually decided to marry her. He had no other wife. Her family was spared.

Dora's life was unbelievably hard but she survived. General Chun was sympathetic to the Communists and the Khmer Rouge led by Pol Pot that took over in 1975. Ultimately, he was given a stipend and he left political life for the shipping business. He soon found it interesting to do a little trading of sorts himself. He made some contacts in Central America and his smuggling business overtook his shipping business.

The business had several branches, including drug trafficking, human trafficking, and even some aquatic trafficking. He did it all.

Dora grew more and more unhappy. She still had family in Cambodia and a son who was being raised separate from her by her family. She begged her husband to let her go. Amara Chun was growing old. He arranged for her to go to California in the United States. She would be under the control of his family but could have a separate residence. She must do their bidding. She had been a good wife. He had no further need for her.

Dora stayed with Amara Chun's family for a time. They grew tired of her and had no use for her. She was allowed to live in a home purchased for her in Pacific Grove.

Unhappily, Fred was her nephew-in-law. He intruded on her exile in Pacific Grove. She allowed him to stay when he had business in town. She had no choice. She watched him closely. She tried to minimize his harm to others.

When she met Lee, Dora was stunned. She did not know there was human trafficking going on as far north as California. She knew her brother-in-law was involved. When she looked at Lee she saw herself at Lee's age. Was Lee to have a life of yearning and sadness? She looked at the young men with Lee. One of them could be her grandson. She may as well tell all. She had lived under the shadow of the past long enough.

The night has passed by on its voyage around the world. It has removed its cape from the world. The dawn of a new day has arrived.

Dora closed her eyes and slept.

CHAPTER XIII

THE DAWN

The first act of Dora's attorney was to remind her that he had worked for her husband's family. He did not work with them on any matter that would remotely touch on this particular case. He did not feel that he had a conflict of interest. Dora agreed with him. He then set up a meeting with the District Attorney's office and the representatives of government agencies involved.

A transcript of Dora's story was made.

"We will have to verify certain aspects of her story, but if it checks out and if she cooperates with us regarding questions that we have regarding the business, she would have a good chance of release with no charges issued," the District Attorney spoke slowly. "I am not speaking for the federal agencies involved."

Dora was ready to help anyway she could.

"The last time I saw my nephew-in-law, Fred, he was in my home. I have informed him that I was horrified by human trafficking and would not help. If he is not staying there, I have no idea where he is."

Fred Chun was trying to be inconspicuous. He walked around mostly at night. He was extremely careful where he spent the night using fairly expensive hotels and motels where he felt safe. A warrant for his arrest had been issued. He knew he had to leave the area and perhaps spend some time in Costa Rica. He believed he would be safe there. His work here wasn't finished but he knew he had to move on.

She had talked. He Knew it. Paula and Preston talked first. Then they must have somehow mentioned her. She had never been in trouble with the law. She must have been in a panic. I cannot imagine her in a cell. My uncle should never have allowed her to come here. The family respected her. Why would they do that? She only brought with her a sense of right that no longer is followed in this world. I need to wait for one more boat. I would like to find out what the guy from New Orleans is doing here. I would like to get Jessie Anthony for costing us so much with her investigation of that incidental murder on a cruise ship. Most of all, I would like to get out of here before they catch me. This time they will charge me with murder. I killed him for good reason. He wanted to take what was mine. I showed him, but now I have very little.

The authorities confiscated the drugs I had stored in her house. I need to get my hands on the rest. The family in San Luis Obispo has it, along with the GPS from the ship. I need to get down there. I need the protection of the family. Perhaps this is not the time for revenge. Perhaps Calvin can handle some of that. Calvin is also being watched so I have to be careful. Besides, Calvin is not that dependable.

Fred decided he needed to make a run for the family in San Luis Obispo. He needed to change his appearance somehow. He always wore black. Fred always wore his trademark black slacks, back shirt, and black leather coat. He decided to brighten up and get rid of the black. Then he needed to find a way to get to San Luis Obispo without getting himself arrested.

Standing on Forest Street in Pacific Grove on Forest Street, in front of the St. Vincent de Paul's store, Fred looked through the window at a red hoodie jacket. Perfect, he thought. Fred dodged into the store. He would also buy a used shirt and slacks. He was feeling better. No one would notice him in red.

LaVerne was in the back of the store, ironing. She looked up and saw him. She had seen the picture that Mary took of him. He was wearing a black leather jacket and black shirt. She dialed 911, stepping back from the doorway. She did not want to tip him off and did not let anyone know who she saw.

The police arrived quietly. There were no sirens. The Pacific Grove Police Department offices are on Pine Avenue, right off Forest Street, within blocks of St. Vincent de Paul. LaVerne was happy. The police walked into the store. Fred looked around for somewhere to run. The customers and staff moved out of the way.

"Fred Chun, you are under arrest for drug trafficking. You need to come with us."

One of the police officers recognized LaVerne and nodded in her direction. Fred Chun was taken out of the store and placed in a squad car. LaVerne immediately called Jessie. The net was tightening on some really nasty people. The town of Pacific Grove was a little safer.

Jessie was thrilled. She told Joe and really felt like celebrating.

"I have really been careful lately. I looked around at St. Angela's. I was afraid to go to the Roasters or to Juice and Java. I am calling a meeting at Juice and Java for this evening. I am so happy."

At Juice and Java that afternoon, LaVerne was treated as a hero.

"You recognized him from the picture I took? That's amazing," Mary said happily.

"I also saw on the web that he was wanted by the police. They had a different photo and they used your photo. I couldn't believe he would come into St. Vincent de Paul's, but there he was."

"You did very well, and I personally want to thank you. A huge weight has been lifted from me. I once again feel snug and safe in my little town. I would really like to know why he was particularly nasty to me. It is really unlikely that I just wouldn't remember him if we had some sort of a court battle. He also mentioned Joe. It is a mystery." Jessie took a sip of merlot. "We need a real meeting with strawberry wine very soon. We have a lot to celebrate."

"I hope that Lee and her friends are given some freedom and that Zeffra Brewer will let us see her soon. I wonder if this changes anything for Dora." Joan said wistfully. "I really hope it does."

Brad heard about the arrest of Fred Chun. He wanted to be at the questioning. The process went along smoothly. Fred Chun's attorney put in a not-guilty plea. The questioning began on a windy, cool, and blustery day in November. Brad took his place in the rear of the room. Fred Chun's plea was discussed at length. The District Attorney made it clear that several agencies were involved and that at the present time he was just charged with drug trafficking. It was highly likely that he would be charged with human trafficking and homicide. The District Attorney warned that it was also highly likely that he was wanted by several other countries.

Fred conferred with his attorney.

"Mr. Chun does not wish to change his plea. He maintains his innocence. As always, he will cooperate with the authorities and answer any questions they may have to the best of his ability."

Brad couldn't help but stare at the man he had known in Louisiana. His appearance really hadn't changed that much. He had a perpetual sneer on his face that seemed to enforce his aura of evil. He had been involved in human trafficking from the Caribbean and from Mexico. He was also deeply involved in drug trafficking.

It was as if Fred felt Brad's eyes staring at him. Fred looked to the back of the room. He saw Brad for the first time. There was a look of recognition that passed.

Brad smiled. "That's right, it's me. Weather is a little cooler here, right? Heard you vacationed in Costa Rica after I left. Louisiana will never be the same without you."

"I was wondering the other day when I saw you on the beach with that girl what you were up to. Now I know that you are one of those sly, cruddy turncoats. You turncoats are the lowest creeps going," Fred said, looking at his hands and making a fist.

"Yeah, I was just wondering if there are any open cases with your name on them down south. I don't know, Fred, but I think you might consider a singing career and sing your heart out to the District Attorney here."

Fred looked at his attorney. His attorney shook his head. Fred decided to be very cooperative.

"My aunt did nothing but see to it that, when I came to Pacific Grove, I conducted my business in such a way as no one got hurt. She learned about the load of people from Cambodia after they were here. She was furious. She wanted to help them. I tried to convince her that they were better off here than where they came from. She would have none of it. She said Lee's family was aristocratic and that she was well-educated. She said that General Amara Chun would have stopped me from using her as a sex slave. My aunt pointed out that the General married her, and I pointed out that Lee has not been touched so far. Virginity brings a very good price. She would have gotten use to her role. This is just a business. I take some pleasure from my charges, but I am not cruel."

"Lee has told us much about her treatment at your hands."

"Our cartels are very large and very powerful. The family living in San Luis Obispo has all but gotten out of the business. The younger members are introduced to the business only if they show great interest. They have become very respectful of Aunt Dora for some reason. The GPS for the boat was hauled there along with perhaps some drugs."

"How closely have you worked with Paula and Preston?"

"They have been flying high for some time. They have been helpful in the selling of drugs. They were scared to death when the accident occurred at Big Sur. They wanted no part of it but it was too late. We needed them. I am sure they broke down and named everyone they ever knew. They have no concept of who is important and who is not important in this business. They really are not part of the business. They helped to give Lee and her friends a sense they had gotten away and kept them where we could keep an eye on them without too much trouble. The house was the perfect place to keep them. No one really went there. We knew when the realtor would be around. Let's just say, we had a system and it was running smoothly until Jessie Anthony and her snoopy friends entered the picture. I couldn't resist trying to frighten her. I know her from a while back. She was on a cruise when a deal was going down. She messed it up. I owed her."

*****

Calvin was at a loss. His world was collapsing around him. Where should he go? He was well aware of the arrests of Paula and Preston. He was aware of the arrest of that bleeding heart, Dora Chun. Now he heard of the arrest of Fred Chun.

How long will it take for them to catch up with me? I have to get away. I love Costa Rica. I could live quite well. The problem with Costa Rica is that the Cartel was there. How long would I survive with them all around me? They might think I knew too much. I would find imprisonment in the United States preferable to life with the Cartel breathing down my back. The best place would be Southeast Asia. I know people there. I could live very well. I even own property there. I could not operate as a legitimate food broker again... but then maybe I could if I kept my name out of it. I might be able to start a new life and even shake off the grip that drugs have on me. There were plenty of beautiful women. I will get out of that business though. It is just too dangerous if I live permanently in Asia. Families sometimes remembered. I could live very well with doing nothing illegal.

But how can I get out of the country? The authorities are looking for me. I've had to leave almost everything in my house. They are sure to come to my house and probably the house at 14 Amber Street. I took what I could. I cannot take my car. They would look for that. I need help getting out of this country. I didn't kill anyone. I am a victim of circumstances. I was a very religious man. After using drugs and alcohol for so long I turned against my religious faith. I became a drug trafficker and a human trafficker. I can give it all up now. I am too old for all of this. My family has disowned me. They shouldn't complain. They used some of my earnings. They didn't ask where the money came from when I gave it to them. They took it and used it and now condemn me as a drunk and druggie. They know nothing of what I have been through. I had never had that kind of money before. In Asia, I could have lived like a king for a long time. I have horrible pain in my head, in my stomach, and in my chest. My family never asked why I lost so much weight. I know I don't have long to live. I refuse to live my last days, weeks, months, or years in custody.

Calvin had been walking along the bike trail. He was wearing a baseball cap covering his bald head. He had panicked and left with his cash, cards, and little else. He was wearing dark glasses, which he hoped would help disguise him from authorities. He walked along briskly. A strong wind had come up and the Monterey Bay had small whitecaps. He noticed her on a bench close to the Monterey Bay Aquarium. She was talking to the young woman he had met at Jessie Anthony's Halloween party. They didn't notice him. He stopped and pondered his next move. He had a gun. He was going to dump it before he went through security if he decided to try to fly out of California. He had never used a gun, but he thought he needed to carry one.

How can I use them? Could they be my ticket out of here?

While Calvin was pondering how they could help him with his escape, Jessie and Belle were chatting and enjoying themselves. They were not volunteering at the aquarium but had attended an enrichment meeting.

"I am so glad he is under arrest. LaVerne really has earned my gratitude. I don't have to keep looking over my shoulder."

"Brad has said he wanted to meet up with me tonight. I know he was at some of the questioning but I am sure that isn't what he wants to share with me. He sounded as if it was important. I gave him the number for my business cell phone so that he could reach me there."

"Hopefully it is strictly personal. I think you two make the cutest couple. You both are enthusiastic about everything and have so much in common. I know you don't want to rush and have some misgivings about the past. I don't want to give advice, but I will. My advice is simply to keep an open mind and don't judge the present Brad by what happened in the past."

Calvin couldn't hear what was being said. He watched as Jessie and Belle stood up to go their separate ways and then he acted. He thought of waiting until they separated and decided that he wanted to use both of them.

"Well, hello, ladies! I am so very happy to see you today! I haven't seen too much of you lately," Calvin exclaimed, walking up to them. "You are both looking well."

Jessie felt her heart sink. Calvin's approach was threatening. She had dismissed him from her mind when she heard about the arrest of Fred Chun.

"Well, Calvin, it is nice to see you out and about. How have you been?"

"I have been busy. There are so many things going on in our little town. I think you know about them. I think you both know about them. Now, you two are going to take a little walk with me. You are not going to scream or call out. You are just going to come with me. You are going to come with me now," Calvin spoke slowly and deliberately. The gun he held under his scarf became visible to both Jessie and Belle.

"What are you doing, Calvin?" Jessie was shocked at seeing a gun in his hand. "Why are you treating us like this?"

"Come on, you two are both involved with the FBI. You know I was a person of interest. After the arrest of Fred Chun, I am sure I am more than a person of interest."

"Calvin, if you are involved, you don't want to make it any worse.

Turn yourself in. You can tell your story to the FBI. If you tell them everything you know, then they will probably give you a break. Do you have a record?" Jessie tried to stall.

"Don't give me that lawyer stuff! I would never see the light outside a prison. I am not in good health. I haven't got that long. Start moving, over there." Calvin motioned to a dilapidated shed close to the water.

"Calvin, why are you doing this?" Jessie asked. "How can this possibly help your situation? What have we ever done to you?"

"Don't act so innocent. You have made fun of me. You have laughed at me. You didn't want me at your party."

"Calvin, that was because you were drunk. Who wants someone that is drunk at a party? Let us go now! Belle has never harmed you or even laughed at you. Why take her?"

"Her boyfriend had that Bureau look. You are both involved with people that could possibly be of use to me. You could also tell them where you saw me. I don't need that. I am making up a plan as I go along. Get in there!" Calvin ordered as he opened the door of the shed.

The shed was located behind some equipment storage buildings on the beach in close proximity to the Monterey Bay Aquarium. The noise from other equipment in the area drowned out any voices.

"I've used this building before for storage of smuggled goods until I could get rid of them. Nobody bothers to come here. No one will look for you here. I have an old van stored down the street. Like the homeless, I move it occasionally. I am going to make a run to the San Jose airport. If anyone stops me, I will let them know that I have you two and your lives depend on my safety. I think a couple of important people value your safety. Let's see now. I have some cables here to tie you with. Let me have your purses." Jessie and Belle handed their purses to Calvin. He continued, as he tied them up with some nylon rope he found lying in the shed,

"I assume your cell phones are in them. Yes, they are. I hope you ladies have a peaceful day and probably night. I will bolt the door. I have the only key. This shed kept my drugs safe. I am sure it will do the same for you. When I am safely on my way to my destination, I may let the authorities know where you are. Then again, I may not. Hopefully, we will *not* see each other again. It has not been a pleasure."

"Calvin, I wanted to ask you something," Belle said, surprisingly calm. "I saw you one day with a metal detector on the beach. You seemed to be looking for something that you had lost. It is so hard to find something in the sand. The sea is constantly piling more sand on top of the existing sand. Did you find what you were looking for?"

Calvin looked stunned. "You ask too many questions," he stammered. "I was looking for my broken heart. I am not going to try to gag you. No one will hear you, so save your breath." He slammed the door as he left. Belle and Jessie heard the key turn in the bolt lock.

Belle and Jessie looked at each other. "Don't worry Belle. I've been in some really rough places before. I've already said several prayers to St. Jude. We will get out of here."

"As long as I can get my hands free or you can get your hands free. We will get out of here. He took our cell phones. Mine is set with the Find My Phone application."

"Mine is, too," Jessie smiled.

"My guess is he will either just toss them or disable the Find My Phone application, if he is smart enough," Belle spoke as she struggled against the restraints. "The good news is that I still have a cell phone. I have my business cell phone in my vest. It also has a Find My Phone application. I wish I could get free. He just tied these cords so tight."

"He certainly did a good job on them. I cannot budge the cords. My wrists are really sore already. The problem is, no one knows we are missing."

*****

Calvin walked to the van, parked where he had left it a few days ago. *Why did she have to ask me that? "I was looking for my broken heart." I was looking for her broken heart. We had a good marriage before I lost myself to drugs and alcohol. I loved her. The other women meant nothing to me. I wanted her back. I wanted my true love back. I sent her the golden heart and told her that she held my heart in her hands. She sent it back and said that I broke her heart and she didn't want mine. I stood on the shore and threw it into the sea. Then I wanted it back. I went to the place on the beach where I had stood when I threw the heart away. I searched and searched. But the sea had accepted my heart as a gift.*

A hand clamped on his shoulder.

"I've been looking for you. You took your time to show up."

Calvin gasped. He felt a sharp pain in his chest, collapsing at the feet of the officer who was going to make him move his van. The officer immediately called for assistance and an ambulance.

*****

Mary tried to reach Jessie. The Strawberry Wine Club was in session at Juice and Java. Her message went to voice mail. Jessie was missed but the meeting went on. Jessie was to report on the progress of the property acquisition. It was not like her to miss a meeting that she had called without any notification.

Mary walked home after the meeting. She was worried about Jessie. She walked passed Jessie's house and saw Joe on the deck.

"Is Jessie okay?" she asked Joe.

"I thought you ladies were having a meeting this evening," Joe answered. "She is not at home. Let me call her." Joe's call also went to voice mail. "That's not like Jessie. I wonder what happened. She was going to meet with Belle early today. I don't have her phone number. I do have Brad's phone number and he has been seeing her. I'll give him a call."

"Please call me when she gets home. I know she is fine, but with everything that is going on, I'm concerned."

"I will certainly do that," Joe answered.

Brad was really worried when he received Joe's call.

"I've called her on her cell phone several times. I called both her personal line and her business line. I got nothing but her voice mail. We were to meet tonight. I told her it was important. This isn't like her, Joe."

"Let's get on it. Let's call the authorities."

*****

Belle was starting to panic. Her phone rang. She knew it was probably Brad. She knew that its battery was low.

"We have to get free. There is nothing in here that's sharp."

"Joe is just now missing me and Brad is missing you. They'll find us," Jessie tried to sound positive. "I would rather not spend the night here, though. It's really cold."

Brad contacted the Bureau. He found out the Bureau had just received the news that Calvin had been brought to the hospital. Authorities had discovered two cell phones in his coat pocket. They each had flower covers. They examined the phones and found they belonged to Jessie and Belle. They did not know if Calvin would gain consciousness.

The authorities scoured the area. Friends of both Jessie and Belle were contacted. There was no doubt that Calvin was involved in their disappearance and yet there was hope that their whereabouts before the disappearance might be a clue to where they were located now.

Brad was able to contact Belle's office. Belle had left early in the day and not returned. Brad tried calling her again on her business phone. The phone startled Belle, who then burst into tears.

Joe and Brad had met up for coffee and an exchange of information.

"I know it's stupid to call her phone, but I don't know where to go except the beach and I don't want to go there."

"I'm not really up on new technologies, but isn't there some way you can locate a phone if you lose it?" Joe asked.

The area was soon covered by officers from the local sheriff's office and the DEA. It had grown dark. Dogs were brought out to help. From within the shed Jessie and Belle started banging on the sides of the shed and screaming. Brad was the first to hear.

"Over here!" he yelled. "I think they are here!"

The others rushed over and the door was knocked down. Brad and Joe were the first to rush in and reach Belle and Jessie. Questions waited for love to express itself.

"Calvin must have been a boy scout," Joe muttered as the officers cut Belle and Jessie free.

"Did you catch Calvin? Did he tell you where we were?" Belle asked.

"He is in the hospital and has been unconscious since he was discovered, quite by accident. No, honey, your phone told us where you were and it was the classic hero Joe Anthony that came up with the thought. When it led us to the beach, I almost lost it. I didn't want to get you involved in anything dangerous, but I did."

"Brad, I got into this myself. I came to Jessie's party myself. We all want to protect those we love but sometimes that's not always possible. You and Joe are both heroes."

"I agree," Jessie said. "I want to get out of here and go home."

"Both of you need to stop at the hospital to have those arms looked at. We can save questioning until the morning," the officer stated. "We will take you two in the ambulance. I am happy to see that you will be able to sit up for the ride."

No argument was made. The evening was suddenly softer and much warmer. The moon had come out and the beach was again very beautiful.

CHAPTER XIV

DON'T GIVE UP

Brad had taken Belle home after being checked over at the hospital. Not to her home but to their home, his home.

"I want you here. I will never let anything hurt you again. I was so afraid I had lost you for good. I had lost you before and was given the gift of finding you. I wanted to tell you that I had worked undercover for the Bureau in New Orleans but I was afraid you would be somehow in danger if I told you. I had decided to tell you last night but then you were taken away from me. I have to tell you now. I have to let you know that I need to spend the rest of my life with you. Please stay with me, now and forever."

Belle allowed herself to be carried to his bed. "I don't have a tooth brush," she said.

"I have an extra one. You don't need any clothes."

Belle snuggled down on his pillow, their pillow, she smiled.

"Watch out for my arms. They are sore. I want you, I need you, Brad, and I love you, now and forever."

Brad held her. "Your arms are the only thing on your body I promise not to touch. I love you with my whole being. This is for forever."

*****

The next morning came with the ringing of the phone.

"I'll be there as soon as I can."

"Brad, you are leaving me so soon?" Belle asked in a sleepy voice.

"Darling, I will take you to your apartment. Calvin is gaining consciousness. I need to be there. I know I could make some things go easier. I love you so much."

Belle was already pulling her clothes on.

"Wait, darling. You didn't shower. We both need to shower. Let's save time and do it together." Brad kissed her on her ear.

*****

Joe and Jessie had spent the evening holding on to each other, as well.

"You are my hero and my love," Jessie whispered.

"You are my life," Joe answered.

Joe received a call from Brad the next morning, letting him know that Calvin was conscious.

"I will definitely try to keep you two in the loop," Brad promised.

*****

Calvin was sitting up in bed. He had suffered from shock. His body had been so abused by drugs and alcohol for years it was ready to quit. Doctors had worked through the night to try to save him. The doctors met with the authorities outside Calvin's room. A guard had stood by his door all night to prevent anyone from coming into the room or leaving the room.

"Gentlemen, I am aware that my patient is under arrest. I would caution that you question him for a very limited time or you will lose him before you can get the information you need from him," the doctor warned. "I would suggest you question him no longer than twenty minutes."

Brad was among those chosen to talk to Calvin.

"How are you this morning, Calvin? There was a lot of concern last night that you were not going to make it."

Calvin eyed Brad coldly.

"I imagine you were concerned. You wonder where your girlfriend is, don't you? Well I would imagine she is rather uncomfortable now."

"Actually, she's taking the day off today, but I think she's just fine."

Calvin looked at Brad through squinting eyes. "When did you see her last?"

"I saw her this morning. She was looking beautiful. I saw Jessie Anthony last night. She was very tired, thanks to you, but she is home and comfortable now, I am sure. Why did you want to do that to those beautiful ladies, Calvin?"

"I was going to let you know where they were when I got out of this country. They would have been a little uncomfortable, but I am sure they would have survived. I've never killed anyone and I am not going to start now."

"You took a lot of chances with Belle and Jessie's lives, Calvin. We can probably stop talking about them right now. I have some questions about Connie Chen. I understand that you had her name in your wallet as a person to be notified in case of your death. She was notified that you were in the hospital and that you might not survive…"

Brad stopped in midsentence as Calvin tried to lurch at him from the bed.

"Don't you dare get her involved in this matter! She has nothing to do with it. She is my former wife. She has never been involved in any of my business dealings. She is a saint, an angel. Leave her alone. I will not allow you to question her. I will not allow you to embarrass her in any way because of me."

"I am afraid I need to ask you to stop the interview right now. You are upsetting the patient. He is very weak," the doctor stopped the interview. "We'll let you know when you can come back into the room."

Brad was surprised by the reaction of Calvin at the mention on Connie Chen. He went to the nurse's station.

"Does Calvin O'Reilly have any visitors scheduled?"

"No, he does not have visitors scheduled. As you are aware, his visitors would have to be approved by the police. There have been inquiries as to his progress made by a Connie Chen. She has asked to speak to the doctor on duty. We have notified the doctors. I do not know whether anyone returned her calls."

*****

Why did I still have her name in my wallet? I am sure she could care less whether I live or I die. She left me a long time ago. She wants nothing to do with me and I don't blame her. She was part of a life I no longer have. I would love to see her just one more time.

I had wandered into this shop on Grant Avenue in San Francisco. It was before Christmas, 1968. I was looking for gifts for my family in Ohio. I knew they would be impressed by gifts from Chinatown in San Francisco. She looked at me from across the counter with her beautiful dark eyes. She was wearing silk. I remember thinking her skin looked like silk. I picked up a silk scarf and said, "It is hard for me to decide. I am looking for a Christmas gift for my sister. Could you show me your favorite one in this collection?"

She chose one with rose flowers and with a blue background. I immediately purchased it. I tried to make conversation but she was very shy. "Do you have any suggestions for my parents?" She walked me over to counters with tea sets and ivory. I saw a beautifully carved statue of a Chinese Buddha that I chose for my father. I also saw some lovely jade jewelry and asked her once again to select the piece she liked. She began to be less shy and actually laughed when I clowned around with a jade earring. I loved her laugh. I haven't heard it in so long.

I asked her if we could go to the store next door for tea when she was allowed to take a break. She smiled shyly and agreed. "I am the manager of this store. My family owns it. I can take a break when I want to take a break. Shall we go?" She smiled.

We sat in a little cubicle in the back of the tea house and bakery. "Please order some pastries for us," I requested. A plate of Wonder buns, soft and warm, containing a sort of sweet and sour pork arrived. Several platters of soft coconut and sugar buns arrived. We had a feast and immediately connected. She told me that her family was one of the first families in Chinatown. She told me that she had never been to Asia. I explained I traveled to Asia quite often for business. "I would like very much to bring you with me some time."

She immediately blushed. "I cannot travel with a man unless I am related to him or he is my husband."

I was very brash. "I am not going to Asia for four months. Perhaps we can work something out before then."

*****

Calvin settled back on his pillows. The doctor and nurse moved around him quickly, taking his vital signs. Calvin's heart was pounding. He did not feel well. He didn't like the way the doctors and nurses were dashing around.

"I want my bed lowered. I don't want to talk to anyone now. I can hardly breathe."

"We will take care of the breathing problems. I am going to insert some tubes and lower your bed. I don't think you should talk to anyone more today," the doctor said cautiously.

"Sorry, gentlemen, my patient needs to rest. His signs are not good. We will see about interviews tomorrow but no more today."

Jessie had coffee at the Roasters with several members of the Strawberry Wine Club.

"I just got an exciting email from Lorelee Mogg. She informed me that the owner of the Amber Street property is unexpectedly coming to town. She is hoping everything could come together very soon."

"How wonderful that would be for everyone. The closer we get to the holidays the harder it is to get people together," Mickey said, sipping her glass of chardonnay. "We are all very happy you are all right, Jessie. We knew it wasn't like you to miss a meeting and not call. Just let us know when any contract needs to be signed."

"I will let you know. Thank you all for thinking of me. I felt your prayers while Belle and I shivered in that shed. After all that, I am still worried about Calvin. He was unconscious for a long time after he was picked up. I understand he is in very bad condition. Calvin really wasn't bad when he was sober. I actually feel sorry for him. His addictions took over his life."

Connie Chen awoke bathed in sunlight in her pretty home. It would be 75 degrees in San Luis Obispo on this November morning. She smiled happily to herself as she rested among her pillows. Then she remembered the call she received the night before. Calvin had her name in his wallet with her information. The doctor informed her that Calvin might very well not survive and that if she wanted to see him alive, she needed to come to Monterey immediately. The doctor also informed her that he was under arrest.

She knew he still cared for her and wanted to be with her. She still cared for him but knew he could not be with her. He would bring her down to the place she was several years ago when she knew she had to leave. She had told him, *"You have broken my heart, both the gold one you gave me and the heart within my chest."* She handed him her gold heart necklace. *"I no longer have a heart that beats for you. I no longer want its symbol."*

Connie was no longer in a hurry to get up and start her day. She would soon be leaving for Monterey and perhaps the last meeting with her former husband. She has filled with dread. They had had a blissful married life at first. Calvin loved showing her the world she had only dreamed about. She remembered her first trip to Asia. It was their honeymoon and all was wonderful. Calvin brought her to the various places in Asia he loved, and even to Istanbul. She had particularly liked Istanbul and its Grand Bazaar. She loved the turquoise water and white beaches where the people built statues out of sand.

As time went on, however, the dream changed into a nightmare. It seemed that Calvin couldn't control his drinking. He then mixed the drinking with drugs and he started to sink lower and lower until there was nothing left of the man she had loved.

Calvin bought a little home for them in Pacific Grove on Amber Street. It had needed some repair, but Calvin promised he could take care of that. She filled the home with beautiful furniture and china, along with Asian fine art treasures. At the beginning, it was wonderful, but as Calvin's addictions progressed it became a prison not a home.

Calvin didn't even try to stop her. She moved south to San Luis Obispo. She was comfortable there. Their marriage that had lasted for years ended in a matter of days. Calvin didn't argue over finances. He gave her the home on Amber Street, with everything in it. He had hopes that one day she would return. Years went by and that did not happen. The house was never repaired. It fell upon sad times.

She had appointed Lorelee Mogg as her realtor. She was not in a hurry to sell. She didn't want to think about it. Recently, there was an offer by a charitable group. She would talk to Lorelee Mogg about it on this trip to say good-by to Calvin.

*****

The sheriff's office and the Bureau received calls from the hospital. Calvin O'Reilly had lost consciousness again. The doctors were not optimistic that he would regain consciousness. Connie Chen was flying in to see him. Did the authorities object to having her visit with him, whether he was conscious or not?

The Bureau and DEA had done a search on Connie Chen as soon as her name was given to them by the hospital. They did a thorough investigation and found no record of her ever being involved with drug smuggling. She was an upstanding citizen of San Luis Obispo. She and Calvin had divorced several years ago and no one questioned could remember seeing them together again. The authorities did not object to Connie seeing Calvin. They would question her later if they felt it was necessary.

Connie Chen called the hospital upon her arrival in Monterey. She was advised there was no change in Calvin's condition. He seemed comfortable for the night. She informed them she would come to the hospital the first thing in the morning. As he was under police guard, a morning meeting worked well for the hospital. They informed her that they would have to notify the authorities of her presence.

The morning was sparkling. Connie spent the night in a bed-and-breakfast in Pacific Grove. She woke early and strolled down to the Bay before she sat down to breakfast. She loved the feel of the sea air on her face. It brought back memories of her life with Calvin in Pacific Grove. She walked by the property on Amber Street and was sad to see her lovely home in its present state. She peeked into a window and saw her furniture. Connie was startled to see that, for the most part, it was just as she had left it so long ago.

She returned to the bed-and-breakfast in time to have a steaming hot coffee with wonderful pastries and fruit. She sat by herself at a corner table in the dining room. Roses in tiny vases decorated each table in the room. She closed her eyes for a moment.

Everything is wonderful on my return to Pacific Grove - the weather, the hotel, the food. Everything is great, except my former husband is dying. A tear ran down her cheek. He has been dead to me for a long time. Somehow, I always had some faint hope that he would receive help. Now, it is final. No matter how bad it got I always knew he was the love of my life. I wonder if he will gain consciousness and see me standing there. I wonder if he would want me to be here.

*****

The hospital was a short drive from the bed-and-breakfast. Cheerful ladies in red jackets assisted Connie as she walked to the main information desk to inquire as to the location of Calvin's room.

"Let me walk you to his room. I believe the priest has just left."

A police officer waited at the door of Calvin's room. The priest was actually just walking out the door as they approached.

"Excuse me, Father. My name is Connie Chen. I am the former wife of Calvin O'Reilly. Calvin had been a devout Catholic in the past. Were you able to give him the last rites?"

"Yes, I was able to give him the last rites and give him absolution. Mr. O'Reilly was semi-conscious at the time. He had asked for a priest."

"Would you please stay with me when I go into the room? I need you, Father?"

"Of course, I will be there for support."

Connie looked at the police officer. "I have instructions to allow you into the room," the officer nodded.

The priest opened the door for Connie. Sunlight streamed through the thin shades. Calvin appeared to be asleep. Connie's heart jumped. He looked so tired and so thin! The nurse was checking his vital signs. *Perhaps I should have stayed. Perhaps I could have helped in some way...*

"May I help you, my dear? Would you like to rest in that chair? It may be some time before he awakens," the priest's voice was comforting. "Calvin mentioned you. He told me that he loved you and that he was sorry."

Connie sat down. She looked at the nurse and asked, "How is he doing this morning?"

"The doctor will be here in a moment. He needs to talk to you."

At that moment, the doctor entered.

"Ms. Chen, I am glad that you were able to come. Mr. O'Reilly took a turn for the worse yesterday. He had been up and talking and then suddenly his heart failed him. He may not regain consciousness again. I think he has a matter of hours."

Connie looked from the doctor to Calvin and was shocked to see he was looking at her. She walked up to him and put her fingers on his lips. He whispered, "Thank you, I love you."

"I love you, too. I never stopped loving you."

Calvin smiled and closed his eyes. He would never open them again.

The priest blessed him. Calvin was gone. The priest turned to Connie. "It was good that you were here. May I drive you home? Can I help you in any way?"

"I am okay. Are you with St. Angela's?"

"I am with St. Angela's. Here is my card. Call me at any time. I will come to you if it is inconvenient for you to come to me," the priest said as he walked Connie to her car.

The news of Calvin's death traveled fast through Pacific Grove. The next morning, Jessie attended mass at St. Angela's. The priest asked that the congregation pray for the happy repose of the soul of Calvin O'Reilly. After mass, Jessie walked to the Carmel Roasters with Mary. The wind had come up and the thought of a steaming Café Americano appealed to both Jessie and Mary.

"So much is happening in our world here and in the world in general. Sometimes things move too fast," Jessie said, taking a deep breath.

Jessie and Mary found a table in the back close to the heater.

"I feel so bad about Calvin. I know that sounds strange after what he put me through, but he was so different when he wasn't high on something. I understand that his former wife is taking care of all the arrangements. I have heard she is a lovely woman. This must be so hard for her. It is as if she lost him more than once."

"I cannot believe how you can be so forgiving, and yet, that is the way we are asked to live our lives," Mary sipped her coffee. "When are we meeting with Lorelee Mogg?"

"Gosh, I almost forgot. We are to meet her and the owner this afternoon at 2:00 p.m. I had better get moving. I'll walk with you."

*****

Fred Chun was surprised at the news that the man he worked with, Calvin O'Reilly, was dead. He was terrified at what Calvin might have told the authorities. He knew that Calvin would not have given out any secrets under normal circumstances, but he also knew that Calvin was very frightened of what the cartel would do to him. Circumstances change when you know you are going to die shortly. Fred knew that Calvin had been very religious at one time. Perhaps he confessed to free his soul. Fred knew nothing of religions. Fred decided that he might have to be more cooperative with the authorities. The cartel might be able to help him if he could get into Costa Rica.

Fred conferred with his attorney, who felt it was his only chance of making any kind of deal with the authorities. He immediately contacted officials so that Fred's confession could be taken. The District Attorney and representative of the FBI would be present and agreed that his cooperation would be taken into consideration.

Fred had worried about the family in San Luis Obispo. He had hoped that they were back in Costa Rica. He was informed that the FBI had already discovered the address of his family in San Luis Obispo and had raided the house, only to find it deserted. Evidently, the family and any smugglers hanging out there had left in a hurry. The police found no drugs but they did find a GPS.

When it was time to meet with the DA and FBI representative, Fred began telling his story again. His uncle, General Amara Chun, had started the business and was very good at it. The company picked up partners in Central America. Human trafficking, drug trafficking, even aquatic trafficking were handled by the family's company. They did some business with groups around the Gulf of Mexico but lately were focusing most of their business along the Pacific Coast as far north as the Big Sur Area of California.

"If the Sheriff's Department of San Luis Obispo County found the GPS of the boat, you already know the route that was taken by the boat that ended on the beach. You already know that the boat stopped for some time in the Sea of Cortez on its way up the coast. The boat was loaded with a drug shipment and we had four people we picked up earlier. The girl, Lee, was to be used in the sex trade. The three men would be used as labor on the boat for a while. Possibly, they would have been used in the sex trade, too. The Super Bowl is to be in Santa Clara. We thought there would be a demand."

Fred took a drink of water and continued.

"The boat stopped in the Sea of Cortez to do some fishing. The crew and the young men on board fished for totoaba fish. A fish bladder from that fish sells for between $7,000 and $14,000. Our crews are not bothered by the fact that the fish is on the brink of extinction. The Chinese pay the highest premiums and sell the bladders for soup that can go for as high as $25,000 a bowl. There are so-called factories in Mexico that handle getting the bladders into the hands of the Chinese.

"I was on shore when the boat landed in Big Sur. We had no indication that the boat had been picked up by the Coast Guard trackers. I quickly realized that the captain of the boat had made his own deal with the Mexican factories. The crew was also not aware of the captain's treachery. It became mayhem on the boat. Knives were flashing everywhere. I stabbed the captain on the shoulder to let him know I meant business. I was pushed aside by a crew member that wanted his money. My assistant helped me round up the captives, including Lee, and the drugs on board. The captives were led to where I knew the Canadians, Paula and Preston, were waiting. I am sure most of the crew members and the contacts in San Luis Obispo are either in Mexico or Central America by now."

"How did Calvin fit into all of this?" the District Attorney wanted to know.

"He was used as a go-between in both Asia and California. His business covered up his interactions on both ends. The girl would have been his first. He had this fixation on his former wife. He heard about Lee and thought that another young Asian girl would fill his need. I would pick up rare Asian art for him from time to time. He saved it for the day his wife would return. Calvin was an unusual person. When he was sober and off of drugs he was almost spiritual. He was driven by guilt. Then, on the other-hand, the drunken, alcoholic Calvin was a lustful thief. I could never trust him. I actually miss him.

"I will give you any names you want. I can tell you they are out of your reach by now. I don't know who killed the captain. I stabbed him but I didn't intentionally kill him. It was not me. He had hopes of convincing us that the Sea of Cortez fiasco was not his fault. He maintained that the Mexican factory was at fault."

"Do you know the location of the Mexican factory?"

"Not really. It is protected by the cartel. I would be surprised if its whereabouts was not known by certain authorities. That's all I want to say right now. You know where you can find me."

CHAPTER XV

THE BEGINNING OR THE END

Lorelee Mogg returned to her office after a short luncheon break. She had picked up pastries from the local bakery and set up a tea service for her guests. She really was looking forward to meeting with the property owner Connie Chen. She also looked forward to seeing Jessie and Mary again.

Connie Chen arrived first and was seated comfortably when Jessie and Mary arrived. Lorelee offered pastries and tea to all and had all the papers ready for signature.

"I am glad that I had the opportunity to meet you ladies. I lived in the house on Amber Street for quite some time. When my husband and I divorced, he signed the house over to me. I now live in San Luis Obispo and for many reasons do not get to Pacific Grove very often. I wasn't sure what I wanted to do with the house and, as you know, it fell into disrepair. I think both my husband and I had hoped that one day we might live in it again. He recently died and, of course, that is now definitely impossible."

"I am so sorry for your loss," Mary said. "Did Mr. Chen reside in

Pacific Grove? I don't recognize the name."

"I took back my maiden name after the divorce. My former husband was Calvin O'Reilly. He did reside in Pacific Grove. Did you know him?"

"I knew him," Jessie stated. "I heard of his death. I also was at St. Angela's for his memorial mass. I was sorry to hear of his death."

"Thank you for saying such nice things. I know he had problems, but he was a good man," Connie said tearfully. "I loved him, and still do."

Jessie and Mary were stunned.

"It is very kind of you to consider our offer. We really believe something needs to be done for both young people and, actually, homeless people of all ages. As the weather gets colder, being homeless is very hard. This is supposed to be a record year for storms. I believe weathermen refer to this type of year as an El Niño year. If we are able to do some repairs before the really bad weather hits, we could help people that need help yet this winter," Jessie said before sipping more tea.

Connie Chen took a deep breath.

"I have been thinking about your offer. It appears to me that you are ladies that are very involved in your community. I have a deep respect for that. You even said kind things about my former husband. Calvin lost most of his fans and I appreciate your words. I can tell you that the house was bought by Calvin and me long before he became involved with anything that was illegitimate. Therefore, I believe the title is free and clear. I know you have limited funds. I know that some of the repairs need to be made immediately in order for the house to be considered habitable. Tell me again what your proposal would be for the use of the house."

Mary jumped into the conversation.

"Several of us have talked with Social Services. They have informed us that they would be more than happy to furnish us with names of girls that could really use a home. We would charge a nominal rent, hopefully enough to pay our property taxes. We do need someone to manage the rents and the property."

Lorelee Mogg volunteered. "I would be able to manage the property if you would like me to manage it. I would consider it my volunteer work."

"That would be absolutely wonderful. I know we could put it together now!" Mary was thrilled.

"The charity really appeals to me. Ms. Mogg, I am prepared to sign over the property to these ladies. I reject their offer of funds. Those funds should be used for the much needed repairs. I will be gifting the property to this charity. Please draw up the papers. We need some help with tax advice," Connie Chen smiled for the first time since arriving in Pacific Grove. "This is the best I have felt in some time. I will enjoy seeing the house after the repairs are made. We will have to talk about the furnishings. I would like to take a walk around the house before I leave. I have given you my keys and left my spare at home. May I borrow one key? I would like to walk around by myself one more time."

"Of course, I understand. I will give you the key and you can return it to me when you are finished." Lorelee Mogg handed Connie a key to her past home.

*****

Connie walked the few short blocks to the Amber Street address. It was a warm late fall day and leaves and acorns were all over the tiny porch. Connie looked at the broken window with glass still lying on the ground. Plastic had been placed over the window to keep out the rain. She wished she had visited the home through the years. The years had passed so fast. She had buried the home as well as Calvin in her heart a long time ago. She had noted that her furniture was still in the room she could see from the window.

The front porch needed repair but could be put in good condition very quickly with a little bit of work. Connie opened the door. She made a mental note that the door needed to be replaced.

After entering the house, Connie pulled out a notebook that she would use to make notes. She wanted to know what furniture and incidentals that she should leave. She wanted to note what articles should be given to St. Vincent de Paul's and what articles needed to be hauled away. She also wanted to note what articles, if any, that she wanted for her home in San Luis Obispo.

Connie surveyed the main room, which included a dining area in a sort of library and sitting area. China was stacked neatly on the side. A lace tablecloth she had purchased so many years ago was still on the table. The library contained books that she had read and books she remembered seeing Calvin read. The linens looked freshly laundered. In the sitting area was a lovely Asian art sculpture she had never seen before; she absolutely loved it and realized Calvin knew she would.

She looked at each of the bedrooms. The beds were made. The coverlets looked freshly ironed. The kitchen appeared to be intact, except for the hole in the ceiling which had been temporarily sealed. The atrium's plants were a little sad but had been watered. The dishes in the kitchen were also stacked neatly on the shelves. Even this late in the afternoon, the room was sunny. Connie was confused. She saw Calvin's hand in all of this but also realized that someone else cared about the house. She had her notes. She left the house and locked the door.

Connie planned to stay another night and realized she could return to Lorelee Mogg's office before 5:00 p.m. When she entered the office, Lorelee was just beginning to clear her desk for the evening.

"Are you finished looking around so soon? I didn't expect to see you until the morning. Have you made notes with regard to the furnishings?"

"I think so. I was surprised to see the furniture in such good condition. Even the linens were clean and fresh looking. Did you take care of all of that?"

"When I first looked over the property at your request, I was startled to see how well the furnishings looked. As you noticed, even the linens were clean and fresh. I realized that it was possibly your former husband. I also realized that occasionally people were getting into the house to sleep. We have a homeless problem in Pacific Grove. I didn't particularly want to inform the authorities because the homeless that were coming were not disturbing any of the furniture or linens. Had they done that I would have informed the authorities. I took over the responsibility to have the inside of the house kept in good condition. I do this for other properties in order that the property looks its best. In real estate, we call that staging. I hope this meets with your approval."

Connie looked thoughtful. "That is fine. A house that is empty may as well be used by someone as long as no damage is done. I look around this beautiful area and am saddened to think of people that are homeless."

"Yes, it is sad. My good friend Wanda writes a column in the local paper, the *Cedar Street Times*, which she calls 'Homeless in Paradise.' She is raising awareness by directing the public's attention to the needs of the homeless in our area. She is a very caring person and has publicized events planned to raise funds for the homeless. I am thrilled to be in a position to help in this endeavor to house these young people on Amber Street.

"Now tell me, what items do you wish shipped to you? I will be happy to make arrangements."

Connie closed her eyes. "I know that Calvin obtained the Asian sculpture for me. I will take that back home with me. I will leave the rest. I would hope some of the furnishings can be used and, hopefully, the other items can be used in other residences for homeless people or they can be used for sale at St. Vincent de Paul's. I know St. Vincent de Paul's gives clothes to the homeless and I believe they do the same with furniture. I know my former husband took from this community. I want to give back in his name."

"You are very kind. Life leads us down many paths. Very few paths are without turns. I hope you keep to the path you are following. You are a very special person," Lorelee said with genuine sincerity.

"Please, give my best to the lovely ladies who are taking care of my former home. I will stop by tomorrow for the statue."

*****

Mary and Jessie were ecstatic upon leaving Lorelee Mogg's office. They called an emergency meeting of the Strawberry Wine Club at Juice and Java.

"I cannot believe we can use the money raised to improve the home! That is absolutely wonderful!" Joan was visibly thrilled.

Mickey agreed. "We can start looking at contractor's tomorrow. All of us have used contractors for various types of work. I think we'll be able to hire some good people at good prices. I believe Augie has a general contractor in his group. Perhaps we can turn the job over to him. Remember, we were going to try to get the tenants to do some of the work."

LaVerne jumped into the conversation. "It would be wonderful if we could use some of the homeless with contracting experience to help. Earning some money for their work would be such a bonus for them. If we could obtain more funds from groups, we could employ more people, including the homeless. It would be a win-win situation."

Jessie raised her glass, "I want to propose a toast to the Strawberry Wine Club!"

*****

The various agencies and the Sheriff's Department of Monterey were in the process of making some big decisions regarding the individuals they had detained. They decided that Paula and Preston had given them all the information that they would find useful. Canada wanted the two for some drug issues north of the border. The United States decided that their prisons were crowded enough and were happy to turn Paula and Preston over to the Canadian authorities.

The various agencies and the Sheriff's Department of Monterey also decided they did not want to pursue the prosecution of Dora. She had not reported crimes or turned in people that she knew had committed crimes. She did not knowingly hide drugs in her home. Her attorney pointed out that there are few laws that demanded one act in the affirmative with regard to reporting crimes. He also pointed out that she had cooperated fully with the authorities. Dora was released with no charges being made. She was happy to return to her home and only wanted to make amends. Dora hoped she could regain the trust of the people she respected. She decided she would not move from Pacific Grove.

Fred Chun, Dora's nephew, was another matter. He had a long history of drug trafficking and human trafficking. He would be held without bail. The prosecution made the case that if bail were set it would be raised. He had no ties to the community and would be out of the country in a hurry. The cartel had a tremendous amount of cash and would post bail to get him out of the country and silence him one way or the other.

Then, of course, there was Lee Hong and her brother Manny. There was also Akara and Bora, Manny's friends. Separate attorneys were appointed for each party.

Lee Hong's attorney was Zeffra Brewer. Zeffra was one of those wonderful people who not only do a competent job but far exceeded any expectations. She was fantastic in the court room and in the research she did. The revelation with regard to Dora greatly disappointed her. She had fostered the relationship that Lee had with the ladies of Pacific Grove and particularly with Dora, who knew Lee's native language and had a connection with Lee's native country.

Zeffra was greatly relieved when she heard that Dora was released with no charges being made against her. She thought about renewing the relationship but decided that could wait until Lee Hong was out of any type of custody. Ms. Brewer spent some time researching the country from which Lee's family came. The country had much political upheaval. She found that Cambodia had an office in San Francisco for the issuance of visas and that they were relatively easy to obtain, at least for a citizen of the United States. She made inquiries within the local Cambodian communities. She decided to do research on Lee

Hong's family and discovered that Lee's father had spoken out against the government of Cambodia and that he had been imprisoned for some time. The records indicated that there was some movement to set him free.

Zeffra used the various agencies that were involved with the case to further her research. She was extremely happy to find that Lee's father was freed. Both Lee's father and mother were allowed to flee to England. They were living there in the Cambodian community. Zeffra wasted no time in giving Lee the fantastic news.

Lee and Manny were absolutely thrilled to hear of the survival of their parents and longed for the day they could reunite with their family. The parents had thought their children were dead. By all appearances, this was to be a fairy-tale-ending to an otherwise tragic story, but as so often is the case, the ending of this story is not so simple.

It was determined that Lee Hong and Manny Hong were victims of crime. Akara and Bora, who were represented by two separate attorneys, were thought to have cooperated with the smugglers after being brought to Pacific Grove. This would slow down the entire process as additional backgrounds had to be checked.

Akara's attorney and Bora's attorney argued that they, too, were victims of crime. They argued that Akara and Bora acted out of fear. The Sheriff's Department had been told by Preston that they had assisted him on a few deliveries. After some legal maneuvering, it was determined that they were also victims and had not willingly assisted in any crime.

Another complication arose when Lee Hong confided to Zeffra Brewer that she and Akara were in love. She volunteered that she remained a virgin and that she would remain a virgin until she was wed, but she had given her heart to Akara. He had been her protector, along with her brother Manny.

Akara had been shackled because he had fought to protect her from a crew member who wanted her for himself. The captain had given strict orders that Lee not be touched because of her worth as a virgin.

The crew member had decided that he needed her and that the captain need not know of his adventure with her. Akara would have none of it and fought with the crew member. When the captain discovered the fighting Akara was beaten and shackled. Lee spoke out in his behalf and revealed that the crew member had tried to rape her. Akara remained shackled for another day. The crew member was not seen again.

Their romance consisted of looks and shy glances. They were both very young and had no real social skills. The social graces were very restrictive in the culture in which they grew to adulthood. Akara spoke only Khmer, but could understand some French. He was taught that it is not acceptable to make eye contact with anyone who was his senior in years or who was considered of a higher social status. Lee, on the other hand, was given the opportunity to learn English as well as Khmer.

Lee explained that the education system that the French brought with them to Cambodia was completely destroyed during the Red Khmer regime of the 1970s. When she and Akara were children in the late 1990s, the educational system had been somewhat rebuilt.

"Akara and I are very seldom alone together. My brother would not allow that. We are, however, in love with each other. He is in my heart. I cannot go to be with my parents in London without Akara. I am very torn. I want in my heart to see my parents, but my heart also tells me I cannot leave the man to whom I want to give my heart. I am confused."

"Life is never simple," Zeffra confided. "We will take it one step at a time. My mother always told me before charging ahead to 'Stop, look, and listen.' You must do that now. If I were your mother, I would like to know a little bit about Akara's background before I allowed him to keep you half a world from me. You were thrown together at a tragic time. Now you are thinking of spending the rest of your life with him. What is his religion?"

"He is Buddhist."

"Are you Buddhist?"

"No, I am Catholic."

"Do you think that in its self would present any problems? Do you know where he wants to live? Does he want to return to Cambodia? Do you want to return to Cambodia? How will you support yourself after the initial benefits from agencies run out?" Zeffra was asking the same age-old questions as a concerned parent.

Lee gave the age-old answer of someone in love. "I don't know the answer to all those questions. I only know I love him."

"Well, we are going to take it one step at a time, as I said before. I want you to talk to your parents. We will look into visas and things of that sort. Many people here care about you. We are going to be very careful so that you are as safe and happy as possible. Have you had much time with Akara, even in a group setting, since you have been detained?"

"No, I have not. We live in different homes. I have barely seen my brother."

"The first thing I am going to work on is getting you together with the men in this group. I will contact the other attorneys soon. I am sure they would want to make these arrangements. Next, I want to set up a means of communication between you and your parents."

"I would like that very much. In the meantime, I would really like to meet with Dora and the other ladies that I have met with in the past. I feel they would help me if I stay here with Akara or even if I stay here without him. They have told me they go to church. I would really like to go to church again. I need some help. I thank you for your help. You are my friend, I know that."

Zeffra Brewer smiled. "You are very much in my thoughts and in my prayers, dear. Do not rush your decisions. I will try to set up a meeting for you and the Pacific Grove group. We will work things out, you'll see. I am happy for you and am excited for your future."

Zeffra Brewer got on the phone as soon as she left Lee. She called Dora first. She had looked at her calendar and felt that a meeting could be held on the next Monday afternoon at two o'clock. She told Dora that she was very happy that her name was cleared. She also told her that she wanted the meeting to include Jessie, Mary, and LaVerne, as in the past. She asked that Dora contact them and get back to her.

"I haven't contacted anyone since I gained my release. I am concerned that I will not be received well."

"Dora, this is the time for you to find out. If there is a problem, let me know. Lee needs you all."

Jessie was thrilled when she heard from Dora.

"I prayed that everything would work out for you. I can contact the others, but I think they will enjoy hearing from you. I cannot wait to tell you how great the housing issue is turning out. We all could use your help."

Dora called the others. They met at 2:00 p.m. in Zeffra Brewer's office. Once again, Zeffra had set out tea and some lovely small scones. Lee was obviously thrilled to see her friends. Dora brought a pretty dress for Lee.

"I actually got this at St. Vincent de Paul's," Dora said. "I thought it would look really cute on you for the holidays."

Lee hugged Dora and then everyone else.

"I feel it has been so long since I have met with my friends. Thank you for visiting me. I love the dress, Dora. You are so thoughtful. You all are so thoughtful. Did Ms. Brewer tell you that my parents are alive? They know my brother and I are also alive and well. I am hopeful that I will be living on my own soon."

"I have allowed you to tell your friends about your parents. I thought that would give you great pleasure."

"Thank you, I am happy to tell you all that my parents are living in London. I want to see them but I want to stay here, if I can. Ms. Brewer has arranged for me to meet with my brother and his friends. Akara and I have decided that we want to marry. I know that is a surprise but we have loved in silence for a long time. We told my brother and he approved. Now we will talk to my parents. I hope they will approve. I am so happy that they are alive to know of my happiness. I will wait until I talk to my parents before I make any wedding plans." Lee's breathless declaration revealed her new happiness.

"Congratulations! I am so happy for you!" Dora exclaimed. "I cannot wait to start helping you plan your wedding. I would love to help pick out the dress. This is so exciting. We have to decide whether we should have a traditional or a modern wedding."

Congratulations echoed around the room.

"Perhaps we should allow Lee and Akara to make some of the decisions," Mary laughed. "What fun this is going to be though! Do you know where you want to be married?"

"I would like to be married at Saint Angela's, the church that my friends attend. Akara is Buddhist and I don't know how that will work. He said he will do whatever I want."

"That is a very good beginning," LaVerne laughed. "Maybe we can help you with some of that. Have you any way of getting in touch with his family?"

"Sadly, Akara thinks his family is lost to him. There is always hope but he has been without them for a very long time. His father was a doctor. His services were needed so perhaps we will find him some day."

"My grandson would be about his age if, in fact, I have a grandson. I will be his grandmother for the wedding. I will also act on your mother's behalf for now until you can get together." Dora wanted to help.

Zeffra Brewer interrupted, "You cannot have all the fun. I want to help."

"I volunteer to taste cakes," Jessie laughed.

"We don't need to rush things. As I said to you earlier, we need to take one step at a time. We are going to try to connect with your parents tomorrow. We have been going through channels. The time differences are a pain but we have a phone call set for tomorrow morning. I believe we can do some sort of international face time. This is going to be a very big time for your family. Your brother, Manny, is also very excited."

"I will have a hard time sleeping tonight. I cannot believe I will be speaking to my parents within a day! I have never been happier. I pray that they will be happy for me."

*****

Morning came with a burst of sun. A shower had passed through the Monterey Peninsula right before dawn. Although there was a promise of more rain to come, the brilliance of the sun helped cheer the morning. Lee and Manny were in the offices of Zeffra Brewer at 8:00 a.m. sharp. It was early evening in London.

Lee and Manny were seated close together so that they possibly could both be viewed by their parents. Lee and Manny let out squeals of happiness as their parents appeared on the screen. Their mother immediately broke into tears of happiness as she viewed the children she thought she would never see again.

"You are back from the dead, my children. Your mother and I have been blessed by the God of all. My heart is very full," their father said, speaking in Khmer. A Cambodian interpreter from the court had been called to Ms. Brewer's office to interpret the conversation. It had been decided that attorneys should be present at this first exchange between the family members to prevent any problems that might occur in the future.

"There is so much to say. There are so many stories to tell. I cannot wait to embrace you both," Lee spoke haltingly. "I have found the love of my life. I want you to meet him. I hope you will accept him and our love."

Lee's father smiled. "I have just been given my daughter back from the dead. I will not deny her or her love. We will talk more. We are reunited now even though we are miles apart. Your mother and I are forever grateful for our good fortune. We love you."

CHAPTER XVI

LOVE DOES CONQUER ALL

Belle had gotten home early and was anticipating Brad's arrival. He had told her that he was picking up dinner and that she needed to do absolutely nothing. She met him at the door with a warm kiss.

"Did you forget something? I have done nothing but I can make you a fantastic omelet if you like."

"No, I have not forgotten anything. I am taking you to dinner at a unique, new place on the beach."

"That sounds fantastic! I have heard nothing about a new place on the beach. I cannot wait to see it!"

Although it was only a few minutes after six, it was quite dark. Showers had again moved in and at times they became a downpour, blown by strong winds. Brad stopped along the street and told Belle to wait as he ran around the car to help her out.

"I have a strong, very large umbrella. It's just a short run." Brad placed the umbrella in front of Belle to keep the rain from blowing into her face. He carefully guided her up the short walk to the door.

"This is really intimate. It really is a small place. What a great idea!"

Belle entered. There was a fire in the fireplace and candles lit the small table set with plain white china. The table was by a large window. The lights were so low that Belle could still see the ocean. The window had not yet become a reflective mirror. "Brad, what's going on? We are the only people here."

"I hoped you would like this. My friend is moving and selling this house. He is on vacation right now and knew I loved it. He suggested that we have dinner here in the hopes you would like it as much as I do. If you do, it is ours. It will be ready for us after our wedding, which I am hoping will take place very soon. I do have a dinner that I picked up and, if it is okay, I have your favorite champagne chilling."

"I don't know what to say. I love it. I don't care what the rest of the house looks like. This window is all I need, the window and you."

"My friend told me we are welcome to spend the night. I really don't want to go out in the rain again."

"I agree," Belle said with a wide grin. "We don't want to catch cold, do we? I love you, Brad!"

"I love you, too!" He paused. "I was thinking dinner could wait. I bought you a new robe for the holidays. I thought I would bring it with me…"

"You think of everything, darling."

*****

The morning brought sun to Pacific Grove and the Monterey Peninsula. Residents ventured out and peeked around the outside of their houses and made sure that at least most of their trees were still standing. Dogs eager to be walked happily came out of their beds. Patio doors opened and wet leaves were swept away. Stores were getting spruced up for the holiday rush and Black Friday. The people of the

Monterey Peninsula, as well as people all over the world, were praying that the festive holiday spirit would somehow wash away the chaos that existed in November, 2015.

Jessie had walked Amber and would actually be on time for morning mass at St. Angela's. She was hoping to see some of her friends at mass and really was looking forward to a coffee chat afterward. She hoped Cathy and Norma, the snow birds, would be there. Fortunately, Mary, Cathy, and Norma were all there.

Jessie wanted to talk to a church council member or the priest about rejuvenating the baby room. Jessie's daughter had mentioned that it could use some sprucing up and Jessie thought she would pass it on. Mary decided to lend a hand. Both Jessie and Mary felt pleased with their reception. They had much to talk about on their way to Carmel Roasters. Kathy and Norma had been informed of the exciting events that had occurred in Pacific Grove before their return.

"We are here in time for the celebrations!" Kathy was always ready to celebrate.

"I am so happy that everything has worked out so well for Lee and her family and friends. The holiday season should be a happy one for all of them. I am also very happy that Dora is so involved. She had a heavy burden to carry for a long time. I am also glad that Belle and Brad are together and seem to be so happy."

"Jessie, you are really a matchmaker," Mary chimed. "They look so cute together, it is hard to believe that so much has gone on since they met again at your Halloween party. Really! Certainly some bad things happened in Pacific Grove, but I am buoyed by the fact that people have moved on and that there has been so much love displayed. Belle and Brad found each other. Lee and Akara found each other. The Hong family found each other. Dora has found peace at last. Connie Chen has also found peace and has brought the hope of the Strawberry Wine Club within reach. So much has happened and it isn't even Thanksgiving," Mary said, smiling. "Love conquers all!"

AUTHOR'S BIO

Jeanne Marie Olin

(photo by LaVerne Ridpath,
edited by Joan Savage)

Jeanne Marie Olin moved to San Francisco in the early 1960s. California soon became her home. After a successful career as a dependency lawyer, Jeanne left the San Francisco Bay Area and moved to the Central Coast of California where she pursued her passion for writing and fun.

Jeanne participated in NaNoWriMo (National Novel Writing Month) for four years and published *Dear Jude* in 2013 and *A Cruise Between* in 2015.

Jeanne has been a guest columnist in the Pacific Grove *Cedar Street Times* and a contributor to the *Nevada Narratives*.

MEMBERS OF THE ORIGINAL STRAWBERRY WINE CLUB

(Photo by Jack Savage)

From Left to Right:
Joan Savage, Kathy McOmber, Mickey Scornaienchi,
Jeanne Marie Olin, LaVerne Ridpath, Letty Valdez,
Norma Buller, Mary Hickey. Not shown: Pat Davis.

BUTTERFLY CHILDREN, PACIFIC GROVE, CALIFORNIA

(in front of the post office)

(photo by Jeanne Marie Olin)

Publication assistance provided by *GSP-Assist*, a service of

Great Spirit Publishing

greatspiritpublishing@yahoo.com

Made in the USA
Las Vegas, NV
11 May 2022

48771886R00096